Juan Makes Lemonade

Giovanni Rosario

ISBN-13: 978-0-9855114-0-1
ISBN-10: 0985511400

Printed in the United States of America.

Published in May 2012

Dedicated to all the Juans and Juanas of the world...

PREFACE

This is the book about my friend Juan, a highly human man with virtues found only in Disney classics and dark secrets found only in the minds of serial killers. Juan does not need introductions, or pity, or rewards, Juan is his own presentation card. Our friendship has been one without contracts, social or personal. It transcends judgment into the realm of awe, panic, and profound learning of the homo sapiens' journey into socialization and all its entrapments of slavery. I have never met a freer individual with so many chains to break. The lessons from his friendship have written his story with the scarring of my heart and the breathlessness of my lungs...

JUAN POPS HIS CHERRY

So Juan, all 14 years old of him, and his testosterone powered everything, goes to the bowling alley with his cousins to shoot some pool. He's not much into bowling since there aren't many of those places in his mountainous country, but he's well versed in playing pool and dreaming about getting laid. He already knows what alcohol does and likes it, and also likes to put that Copenhagen stuff in his bottom lip. If it weren't for the racist ways of some of them against black people, these rednecks wouldn't be so bad. I mean, they like to party, fish, and their women really spicy; Just like his people, without the racist part. Not all were racist, but it was a prevalent attitude that was taught to them since they were small. I mean, he didn't even know what the n word meant, so he would go with his female friend who referred to black people using the n word, to the part of his Florida school where all the black people hung out and asked her while walking through them if this was the "nigger" corner. He didn't think anything of it, shoot, he guessed he was one of them too because half of his family was black as an eight ball. It wasn't until later in his life that he understood what that word really meant and all the suffering it caused. He also later understood that Puertoricans were considered a step above blacks and Mexicans, and many steps below white people. Weird people, he thought, thank God they went to church!

Anyways, back to the cherry popping it is. He is playing pool and all of the sudden notices this cute little white girl looking at him with a smile. She's sitting down on the floor wearing a little yellow pair of shorts and very beautiful blue eyes. He walks over and starts talking to her. She has a British accent, which makes her even more interesting. They keep talking and she asks him to walk her home. He, of course, agrees and tells his cousins that he will be back after he walks this girl home. They walk together to a wooden dock by the river close by and start to kiss. They end up on the wooden floor with their pants down. He opens the little packet with a condom in it and it turns out it was not lubricated. It didn't matter, shit!, Juan was so happy he wouldn't have cared if all he had was a Ziploc bag to put on his buddy, he was popping his cherry tonight! A few strokes and he was seizing like an epileptic and was no longer a virgin, yeehaw, God bless America!

After taking the girl back to the bowling alley, they exchanged phone numbers (Juan didn't really know about social contracts that require that you get the number before the nooky) and parted ways, not without first finding out that the girl was not British; like he cared!, she was beautiful and had made him a non-virgin, that's all that mattered to handsome Juan.

JUAN MEETS THE LOVE OF HIS LIFE

Juan used to hang out by the university, where all the students gathered on Thursday nights before leaving for their hometowns all over his island to spend the weekends with their families. He had friends from many walks of life, including the music world. He had become the go to guy in the street for anything from weed, to coke, a girl, a boy, a ride, you name it. The one thing he had realized is that all this moments he was chasing after, that were supposed to be his cherished moments of the future, were nothing more than an attempt at burying his loneliness in others passions. I mean, here was this Greek god figured 21 year old with a very high I.Q. for whom the most important thing was to do as much damage to life as fast as he could, period!

He is leaning against the wooden light post in front of the street bar where they sell the cheap liquor and beer he requires to lube his wits. The jukeboxes are playing some old school salsa and the cars are passing by with a promise of the unknown. He glances up and down the avenue to trawl for opportunity and to be seen. He hears the twin honks from a red four door with two girls and one guy in the car. My kind of math, Juan thinks. It's his girl from the music school, along with two friends looking for a good time and some company. He climbs in the back laughing and happy as a pig in shit. You see, this was a true friend looking to have some fun and share some of her friends with Juan and that made him very happy. He was also happy with the fact that they had some Black Tower wine with them. Mmmm, his favorite! They drive to the 500 year old walled city with the windows rolled down and giggling their life away through them. All throughout the trip to the city Juan could not stop looking at this gorgeous girl that his friend had brought along. She had long brown hair with highlights, killer hips, the smell of flowers, and a smile that could sink a battleship. My God!, was she amazing or what? Juan thought he was just gonna put another mark on his conquest book but boy was he in for a taste of hard knocks liquor. Ooh doggy! To this day he still can't forget that first kiss behind the city wall, in front of San Juan bay with all the stars glistening on the water. It was magic. He ran his fingers through her hair and kissed her lips, and her cheeks, and they tasted the salt in the air mingled with the fire of their souls. Her name was Lucia and Juan was crazy for her instantly. They didn't know it then, but they were in the presence of love, the one and only, true God...

JUAN, THE SON OF CANCER

His mother barks obscenities at him while asking for some sugar. Like a little soldier, he runs to the kitchen to put chunks of papaya in the blender. The coldness of knowing his mother's death is near runs through his soul. But now is not the time for fear, it's time for war; the war to raise his mother's blood sugar. He adds sugar to the papaya smoothie inside the glass blender and starts it up with desperation. Chunks of fruit splatter on the green counter, which matches the green Italian Doric style tiles and the green Osterizer. His mother loves green. She continues to spew fire from her mouth but he knows not to let any of these words hurt him; it's the chemotherapy that's destroying every cell of his goddess' body. She has already told him; "do not take anything I say to heart when my sugar drops, It's not me". He loves her even more at this moment because he knows how much she needs him now. His iron willed stepfather is not at home right now so he has to be the man of the house until he gets home, even though he's just nine years old. With nerves of steel he searches for a glass to pour the smoothie he just made in a hurry and with terror, but above all with love. With the purity and the strength of a child's heart that spits on the face of the monster called cancer, every time it tries to scare him, he runs to his mother's room where she lays on her round bed, shaky and bathed in cold sweat. He helps

11

her hold the glass and drink the shake; he gives her his strength, his soul. She drinks to survive, he gives her a drink to save her. Like he had poured a miracle in the glass, each gulp she takes carries his hopes that the love he poured in the blender will save his goddess' life. His mother's blood sugar rises as he holds and hugs her while wiping her tears from her face. She is crying because she screamed at her son. He's happy, because just for today, he has made his mother feel better. She tells him to get ready because she doesn't have long to live. He tells her that she's never going to die; "you are Mami, you're never going to die..."

JUAN'S CHILDHOOD IN THE MOUNTAINS

When Juan's mother divorced his father they moved to the mountains in Puerto Rico, where her family was from. Juan's maternal grandfather had built a reinforced concrete house with his own hands. He had been an electrician who was very smart and had very little formal education. He was also a chronic alcoholic. When he was young he got run over by a car and this made him incapacitated and depressed. He also liked to gamble, but was a very respectful and decent man. If he owed you money he would pay on time no matter what. Juan remembers living in the house with his mother and grandpa and hearing his screams of pain at night. His back had been broken by the accident and pain was a daily chore of his. His grandpa also did not believe in going to doctors, so when he needed a tooth pulled he would just call his niece's husband to pull the tooth with a pair of pliers and Puertorican rum as anesthesia. He only ate smoked fish, which made him stay thin. His favorite cigarettes were filter less Pall Mall reds, which made his room smell like a cheap brothel. It was not a big deal for Juan, he loved his grandpa and his grandpa loved him. He always made fun of his grandpa's socks, which he said smelled like cheese. In the porch his grandpa always had pinball machines that he used to fix and Juan would get the keys so he could play with them. Usually, Juan could find his grandpa playing craps on the sidewalk by the neighborhood bar. His grandpa would always give him a dollar to buy candy with and Juan was happy.

The farm where Juan's family lived was a 15 acre piece of land left to the heirs of Juan's great grandfather. They had all built their houses there and had a bunch of kids. Juan was always playing with his cousins. Their parents always went to the river that bordered the farm and took food and prepared it on fires they started with wood they got from the surroundings. There were all kinds of tropical fruits and vegetables in the farm. Acerolas, red pears, almonds, avocados, guavas, passion fruit vines, lemons, oranges, mandarins, sugar cane, mamey, and many exotic sweet fruits. It was heaven after school. They would all climb the trees and eat the fruits straight from them. Juan and his cousins drove their parents crazy by climbing all the way to the top of very tall trees to get the best fruit. Sometimes they would collect a bunch of fruit and talk to the owner of the neighborhood store and sell it in the corner, right in front of the tobacco factory. Back then Juan could buy hard candy for a penny a piece, so all the money he and his cousins made from selling fruit they would use for buying candy. The kids always played hide and go seek in the farm at night during weekends. Birthdays were always full of kids and presents from everybody. During the Christmas season the men would kill a pig or two and put them on a long pole and roast them over a homemade coal pit made with homemade charcoal. Juan remembers his godfather making "chimbas" to make natural charcoal. His godfather would gather local timber and make a little mountain with it. He would then take foliage and hay and cover the wood with it. After that he would light the mix of green and dry vegetation on top of the wood. The mix had to be right for the charcoal to come out good. Sometimes Juan's godfather would take three days to make the charcoal. He would then bag it in sacks and sell it. This charcoal brought out the best flavor in anything it cooked. The pole used to go through the pig had a steering wheel or a wooden plank on it to turn the pork with. The adults would put a couple of loafs of bread on a tray under the pork when it was almost ready and the bread would collect the seasoned juices dripping from the pig. It was heavenly! They would start cooking the pig early in the morning and it would take a good eight to ten hours to properly cook. Throughout this whole process someone had to constantly turn the pig so that it would cook evenly. This was usually the job of the kids and they took pride in it. It was an honor to turn the pork for a shift or two. The men's job was to kill and prep the pork. This entailed stabbing it with a knife and collecting its blood to make blood sausage with, and then gutting the pig. The internal organs were discarded except for the intestines, which were used to make sausage with. They were cleaned by the women and then filled with blood, cooked rice, and seasonings. The men would boil water and stick the pig in it to remove the hair from its skin with the help of a knife. After removing the hair they would then make a bunch of holes all over the pig to stick a special seasoning in it. The pig was then ready to stick on the pole. After it was cooked, people would usually fight over the tail, Juan never knew why, but he guessed it was a tradition. He was not crazy about the tail but he really liked the "cuerito"or skin, it was crunchy and full of intense flavor. The family would always enjoy the feast together, everybody pitched in and they all enjoyed a nice Christmas together. It was like living in this fantasy village where the whole community took care of the children and they were all related.

The older cousins would sometimes get ball bearings from auto repair shops and fabricate wooden carts that they would use to ride down the paved hills of the farm. They would use their feet and some rope to steer them as best as they could. The bearings were made of steel so they would slide on the pavement if steered too hard. It took a lot of skill to drive these carts. They used a two by four attached to the cart as a manual brake that would grind against the pavement and stop the car. They would also make their own kites using the ribs from the palm leaves and either newspaper or plastic bags. They would use strips of fabric made from old rags to make the tail of the kite. When it came to spinning tops Juan and his cousins would buy them at the store and remove the little tips that they came with and custom fit wood nails to them. They had to balance the tips just right to get the tops to spin smoothly. In order to smooth the tips so that they would not hurt their hands when they picked them up from the ground to spin on the palm of their hand, they would spit on a concrete surface and grind the tip on it. Juan and his cousins would spend hours after school and on weekends playing with their spinning tops. The kids also played basketball, tag, and fished for rock shrimp barehanded.

Juan learned from the elders how to identify the different edible roots and vegetables that grew in the farm as well as how and when to plant and harvest them. All of Juan's cousins could live off the land if needed. They could all kill a chicken, a goat, and a rabbit and get them ready to eat. Juan's elders also taught the kids what plants to stay away from and which ones cured different illnesses. Juan remembers his mom making him orange leaf tea for his colic when he was a really young boy. They never failed. Later on he developed boils under his arms when he reached puberty and his nanny put some wild tomato leaves with olive oil on the boils. The next day they came to a head and she squeezed them out. It was very painful but they never came back. Juan remembers that when he reached puberty he started getting horny. His older cousins had some black and white porn magazines hidden in an old discarded washing machine behind the farm. They would sometimes go on little jerking off expeditions. Juan thought they were the only ones doing such a thing but he later found out that all boys do it. He just loved his little black and white porn magazines full of bushy haired women. It's funny because Juan jokes about stuff like that today. He tells me he wishes he could still jerk off to the underwear section of the JC Penney magazine, he says he needs way more than that to get going these days. LOLOL. Juan, always honest, always free... All the cousins were like brothers, and even though they fought a lot they would never let anybody mess with them that wasn't family. The elders made sure they taught all the kids how to defend themselves. They got the kids some boxing gloves and put them against each other according to age and size. Juan did not know how to defend himself when he was a little boy and always ended up resorting to biting. His cousins would pick on him until they got him furious and he then would fight all of them as best he could. When he learned how to defend himself he started punching them hard and earned their respect. I guess you could say that bullying was not a bad thing those days, it was a tradition used to toughen up the kids. I'm not sure I would approve of it these days, but it did make Juan fight back. Some kids are not as strong as Juan and all they have to show for are emotional scars as adults. When the kids got a little older they started experiencing their sexuality with each other for a little while, only because they could not get girls, which is what they really wanted. When they got into their early teens they started developing into bigger boys and could now have girlfriends to mess around with, so they focused on that. Juan was ashamed about his homosexual teen encounters for a for a long time but later found out that it is common practice, especially in cultures that have been scarred by religious fanaticism like his Latino culture. Juan explained to me how these religions make a natural thing like sex into a sin, threaten everybody with eternal fire up their ass if they don't follow their rules, make them pariahs if they have children out of wedlock, tell them that using condoms is a sin and say that that God is punishing them after they get HIV from not wearing condoms, don't let them get divorced, judge them and their children if they do, expel them if they talk against their practices, don't let them marry black people, host annual hooded parades with matching color torches and burning crosses, vote for the most racist candidates (upon request from their filthy rich pastors who predate upon every poor uneducated community), burned people alive for not believing on their religion, castrated young boys with beautiful voices (to keep their voice high pitched), murdered every Muslim in their path(who then returned the favor and still do so), killed gay people, sold passes to heaven, prohibit women from serving in positions of power in church, raped children(which would not happen as often if they let priests marry) entrusted to them by their parishioners (and had the pope cover it up), and pretty much led every genocide in the history of man. I was a little concerned with Juan's hate for organized religion but who can argue with him?, he speaks the truth. Juan tells me that he loves what Jesus did but is terrified of his followers, and I don't blame him either, Jesus Christ! A lot of Juan's family members were Christians, some were catholic, some were protestant. Juan was baptized in both churches, first in the catholic when he was a baby, then in the protestant when he was a teenager. His mother was a believer and she wanted the best for Juan but she never forced anything on him when it came to religion. She told Juan how she had left her body during one of her cancer operations and had traveled down the tunnel with light and heard the beautiful music and seen the bright light that didn't hurt her eyes and had spoken to some being that told her it was not her time yet. Juan believed there was something that moved the universe and that gave life but he did not believe in the concept of a guy shoving lightning bolts up people's asses when they fucked up. He just wished there were more people focusing on love and not judgment. Juan developed a deep disdain for organized religion when his adoptive parents became Jesus freaks. They were just normal cool people when Juan's mother died. They did not have children and all of the sudden they had two and converted to heavy duty Protestantism. Juan did not like it because they spent all their time in church. Monday, Tuesday, Wednesday, Thursday, Friday, Saturday, Sunday. The trips to the beach became fewer and everything had to do with the church. He rebelled against all their rules and new found faith. All he wanted to do was experience life, chase girls, get laid, and have a beer. The only problem was that he was fourteen and all those things were frowned upon by Christians at any age. Juan felt trapped, suffocated. He loved his adoptive parents but they did not know how to parent a teenager. They were just doing the best they could with what they had. They did not know about not pushing a teenager because they push back with rebelliousness. They did not know that forcing religion on young people actually put them at greater risk for drugs and running away from home. Teenagers, Juan tells me, are like water in an enclosed place; if you put too much heat on it and don't give it a relief valve they blow up and destroy everything around it. Juan told me he never blamed his parents for him becoming rebellious, that's just how it worked out for him. The trauma of losing his mother at such a young age had not surfaced but when it did it came out with a vengeance. His adoptive parents tried to give him everything they could and to protect him from his father's claws but it didn't work, Juan blew up and left to live with his father for about five months. I think that's when Juan's childhood ended. Nowadays he looks back and tells me he wished he had handled it better, but he's not sure he could have. Juan has been impulsive and incapable of compromising his beliefs ever since I met him. His childhood in the mountains will always be his anchor, his happy place, the memories that carry him through the sea of lemons that rain on him. Juan keeps a couple of houses in his family farm where he can go whenever he wants. He's part owner of one of them and heir to another. His auntie refuses to rent the house he owns even though Juan told her to do so so she could keep the money. She wants to always keep it there for when Juan comes over with Lucía, Brenda, and María and all the kids to visit. It's Juan's childhood home, no matter how rich or poor he is, his childhood home will always be there for him.

JUAN GOES TO LA PERLA

Back when Juan was living in Old San Juan and working as a bartender and server in one of the restaurants facing the Atlantic Ocean, he liked to smoke a joint sitting on the 500 year walls of the city while looking at the La Perla slum and the waves crashing on the rocks. La Perla had been a slum for hundreds of years. Many workers who serviced the rich people who lived inside the walls of the city had settled there, between the northern part of the adobe city wall and the waves. It was a hundred and fifty yards from the wall to the sea. In that cliff about three thousand people lived. Many of them built their little shanties really close to the other and lived in relative harmony with each other. There were a few different sectors within the slum and the people who were born and lived there experienced a type of rebelliousness and freedom only seen in revolutions against empires across the globe. Many famous musicians and percussionists were born in La Perla. The Afro-Antillean slave musical and religious traditions never died in La Perla. When a baby was born to one of the musicians or Santeros of the barriada, a three day music offering to the Santos always took place to offer the child to the African Gods that had protected the slaves' ancesters for thousands of years. The men of La Perla were notorious for their bravery and ferociousness. A butchery had operated at the foot of the hill that touched the sea and the butchers would throw the leftovers into the water. This would bring in the tiger sharks of the Atlantic, along with the bulls. Both species were notorious for their aggressiveness and their man eating habits. The men of La Perla would wait for the sharks to come in and would then jump into the water with spears and homemade harpoons tied to a strong rope and daggers and hunt them with nothing but a pair of flippers and a cheap diving mask. They would harpoon the sharks while they were in the water and the rest of the men would wrestle the shark out to butcher it. It was a sight to behold.

La Perla had its dark side too. Like any slum, illegal activity was one of the main sources of income. Most of the neighbors had little or no formal education, so they had to resort to manual labor and the few trades they had picked up from their parents and neighbors. Unemployment was very high so they did what was necessary to feed their families, including bootlegging, stealing, gambling, prostitution, and drug trafficking. You could go to La Perla to bet on an illegal cockfight, have a few drinks of Pitorro (Puertorican moonshine), hire a hooker, and score some dope. You could even go to one of the shooting galleries to get off, if that was your thing. Justice was swift street justice in La Perla too. If you crossed one of the drug lords or the people who controlled the vice, after you had been warned and roughed up a couple of times, you were liable to get killed in broad daylight.

Juan went down to La Perla to score some weed one Sunday afternoon. He went to the weed dealer in the middle of the little plaza and bought a five dollar bag of natural weed. Back in those days there was no genetically modified weed, it was all natural. You could roll ten nice size joints out of a five dollar bag. If you really wanted to buy more you could get a half an ounce of good weed for fifteen bucks and roll forty joints out of it. If cocaine was your thing you could buy a gram for twenty bucks or an ounce for three hundred. Good, cheap dope, they sold it in La Perla, that's why Juan went there. Juan sat down on a concrete bench and rolled a joint out of his newly purchased bag. He sat and took a couple of tokes and exhaled. The calming effect of the weed started taking effect and the salt in the sea air tasted sweeter, he felt it cooling his Puertorican skin, his universal soul, and quenching his loneliness. A few seconds later the door to the main shooting gallery burst open. A man and a woman were carrying a guy by the hands and feet. His head was hanging as if he was dead. He had overdosed on heroin. They had shot some saline solution into his veins to raise his blood pressure and counter the blood pressure lowering effect of heroin. It was not working; the part of his central nervous system that controlled his respiratory center was almost non operational, so he was not breathing. They laid him on a concrete bench across the shooting gallery and took his shoes off. The man grabbed a two foot two by four piece of wood and proceeded to smack the overdosed guy's bottom of the feet four times. Juan could hear the loud dry sound produced by the strikes on the man's soles. After the fourth time the guy took in a deep breath and came back to an unconscious yet breathing state. The people picked him up and sat him up by a wooden utility pole and dumped a bucket of water on him. He would take deep involuntary breaths every couple of seconds and looked like he was going to make it. A few seconds later, the dealer who sold him the heroin yelled out; "I got that shit, come and get it!". Addicts holding out for a good bag of smack came out of the woodwork to buy the poison that almost killed the guy in the gutter. It was surreal. Juan did not understand it, by then he was not deep into his addiction yet, and such behavior did not make sense to him. He went to the dealer a couple of minutes later and asked him why the junkies reacted like that. The dealer told him that that's what they wanted, to almost die. Many years later Juan became familiar with the concept of wanting to get super high without dying, it dominated his life at the end of his addiction. People who have never experienced addiction will never understand, tells me Juan. He always tells me that being addicted is like having a mistress with a killer body, gorgeous face, and a deep masculine voice, you wanna fuck the shit out of her, just never hear anything from her.

JUAN THE MULTITASKER

Poor Juan had gotten hooked on some drugs. He was walking the streets homeless, stinky, penniless, and hopeless. I mean, he was doing things to get money to get high that he thought he would never do. Stealing, pimping, whatever it took. He tried to stop but he couldn't. Some of the stuff he was doing to get high made him feel so bad that he had to get high to forget about the things he had to do the night before to get high. The end of the movie he was making about himself on drugs was a really long one. It must have lasted five years, but to him it seemed like an eternity. He was tired, it had stopped being fun a long time ago. He had compromised his integrity and thwarted a beautiful future in exchange for a cocaine and alcohol buzz. Bacchus had proved to be a very expensive and merciless god. He knew he still had gifts in him that made him special but he had stopped believing that he could do anything with them, other than feel the regret of never being able to use them.

Juan had been baptized in both the catholic and the protestant church. His mother was a loving single woman who worked as a florist, store clerk, and craftswoman who specialized in ceramics and painting. She was good, really good, but never really had time to develop her talents into a successful business because she developed cancer in her early twenties. She had divorced Juan's father when Juan was two years old and stayed single until Juan was eight. Juan's father had turned out to be a deadbeat, telling everybody how he took good care of his son, but in reality he was squandering his fortune as a businessman by sending his mistresses to college and showering his friends with gifts. All the while, his son had to wear shoes one size bigger and with paper in the front so that he could grow into them. When Juan's father sold the family house where they lived, he made Juan's mother a check for her share of the money and bounced it. Many years later he would also charge Juan 90 dollars to cash one of his student VA checks. Juan's father also tried to sell him some cars that his brother (Juan's uncle) had given to him for free on top of trying to get Juan to tow them across three states. Juan never understood how a human could be so evil, but it toughened him up and he turned that pain into a desire to be a good man, miles from the person his father was. He was really hurt by his father's evil ways, especially when it came to his greed and his hatred for Juan's mother's family. Juan will never forget how his father called his godfather's son the day after his grandma's burial. Juan's father told him to tell Juan's stepdad to send him a plane ticket to go to the wake. In essence he mocked Juan's grandma's death. Juan was in Puerto Rico when this happened and he thought about flying back to Florida and emptying his 18 shot nine millimeter in his father's mouth. He never did though, he knew that the best thing you could do was to sever ties with people like his father and never look back. Even when Juan's father was in his deathbed at almost ninety, Juan refused to go see him so as not to upset him. He really wanted to tell him something hateful, like "hurry up and die so I can take a dump on your grave", but he did not; he forgave him and set himself free of the hatred his father had planted with his actions. So, needless to say, the relationship was never good between the families. Juan's mother's family hated his father, and his father's family believed his father's lies. In the meantime Juan had to rely on the love of his mother's male relatives to fill the void of not having a father. Maybe that's what pushed Juan into drugs and the streets to begin with. But Juan was tired of living this hell in the streets. The crack houses, the shooting galleries, the waking up with strangers who hired him and his friends for some company. The waking up broke in abandoned buildings without a shirt or shoes, even though he was wearing them when he passed out. Having to beg for money from his friends to give to his imaginary daughter that he used as an excuse. The having shit himself without knowing it until his ass burned like a torch. Juan had become a bum, lumpen if you will. He still had his sex drive though, and whenever he scored some money he would visit the local brothel for some good Venezuelan or Dominican women; he couldn't get enough of it. Sometimes he would buy three different women in one night. There was one Venezuelan girl he really liked, even though he met her only once. Juan could tell she was really fighting not to have an orgasm when they were together. Female prostitutes were taught to do whatever it took to not orgasm, so that they wouldn't fall for their Johns. Juan knew that people thought prostitutes were heartless, evil people, but nothing could be further from the truth. He knew a lot of these women had the deepest and most honest souls of all humans. They would trade anything for a good loving husband or wife, a family, and a good decent income. It's just that life dealt them a hand that left them no choice but to fight back with what they had. They were honest; Juan paid them and they serviced him, period! There was no ulterior motive, there were no lies, no promises of eternal love, no pre-nups, no alimony threats, no backroom deals with the state attorney to drop the bogus domestic violence charges in exchange for the house, a car, custody of the kids, and a big fat monthly check. They weren't trying to get you to adopt their kids to later divorce you and get child support from you, even though you were not their father. Juan respected prostitutes for that.

Juan had met many characters during his run on the streets. They all had a story, they all had a dream. Some were actors, singers, disgraced cops, fallen politicians, former athletes, college professors, sons of pastors, disgraced aristocrats. All of them fallen angels.

Juan and his friend Enrique, a former pro basketball player, had taken over the Pan-American village buildings that were left abandoned after the Pan-American games of 1979. The company that had been providing security to stop people from vandalizing the property went bankrupt and left the complex without security. Juan and Enrique saw the opportunity and started opening the apartments, refurbishing and selling them to illegal immigrants from the

Dominican Republic. Juan was the contractor and Enrique did the sales. If Juan needed anything to fix the apartments that Enrique had sold, he had units used solely for parts. For five or six hundred bucks you could get yourself an apartment with three rooms, one bathroom, a balcony, on the seventh floor, with a view to the lagoon. The building's elevators were broken, so the higher floors commanded more money because it took the police longer to climb the stairs to get to you. Location, location, location!

The reason the government couldn't resell the properties after the games was that they were smack dab in the middle of two of the most violent and dangerous projects in the island; nobody wanted to buy anything there. The place was so bad that sometimes Juan came home and the power box breakers from inside the apartment had been stolen, or the water meter contraption he used to steal the water had been stolen. One time he went out partying with some friends who lived in the complex and when they returned all the furniture and the toilet were stolen. Juan would charge people 40 bucks to jack the water for them and 40 to jack the electricity. He would take heavy gauge electrical wire and go to the building's electrical panel and, with a pair of pliers in his bare hands, and plenty of alcohol in his blood, connect the wire to the live circuit. Sometimes, when he hadn't had some alcohol and he was too shaky and scared to taunt death for 40 bucks, he would just shut the entire building's power down to connect power to one apartment. When he would come out of the power room in the first floor all the women were out on their balconies cursing at him for shutting down their stoves and appliances. It was almost comical, and it also provided for steady income because every couple of months the power company came and pulled the makeshift fuses that Juan had installed and people called him to install the power again. Some of the neighbors had plenty of firepower hidden in their apartments, so, whenever the kids from the neighboring project would come to steal a car, Juan would tell them to leave so that they wouldn't get shot at from the balconies. Juan knew the guys from the projects next door because his cousin and his family ran the dope dealing spot, so you could say he had some protection. Sometimes he would get some 5 dollar bags from his cousin, take them to college town and sell them for 20 dollars and still have some yeyo to party with. He really loved the fast lane. Whenever things would get hot in the club he would give the stash to his friend, who was dating the head cop of college town, so he would be clean in case of a frisk or a dime drop. This kid dated some killer women and bagged them so easy, Hollywood couldn't write such a fast story. On one occasion he slept with three girls that were all best friends amongst themselves, lived in the same building, and in the same weekend. They all told each other and laughed.

When Juan didn't want to stay in his place, he would go to the tourist area with his gay friends. His friend Carlitos had a sugar daddy that was a doctor and had a really nice place by the beach. Juan would go and stay for the weekend and they would drink and smoke and toot til the morning came. Driving around the city partying and happy. Pepito and Enrique would come along and Carlitos would take his sugar daddy's BMW and they would all ride around the tourist area like kings of the avenue. It was a site to behold; such debauchery!

On one occasion Juan was offered to get paid for a blow job by one of his college professors. Twenty one dollars he said he would give him. It sounded good at the moment, Juan was stone broke and he could drink all he wanted for free. He would need to because just the thought of it was repulsive to him; Juan was straighter than God but was broker than hell. Swig; down went the fourth shot of expensive sherry along with his pants. He sat there on this guy's bed waiting to finish so he could get out and get high. He swore he wouldn't do that again, but of course, life has a price for everything, including dignity. It was just a matter of time before the opportunity to be broke, a gorgeous male, and jonesing for cocaine and alcohol, presented itself again. It became a steady source of income for Juan, and also a river of guilt, deception, and remorse. It was the most expensive easy money he had earned. Not because he thought anything wrong of homosexuality, but because he had become a slave to his dopamine receptors and he felt dirty for that. Once in a while he would try to sell some dope or steal a car and use it as a dope taxi for hire but all those options took too much planning and risk, he thought. Tricking was quick, physically painless, and he had control of the situation. If he knew of the emotional and psychological scars, he might have done it anyways; the 800 pound gorilla holding a rear naked choke on him felt invincible. He got invited to do burglaries and car-jackings but he wanted nothing to do with violence or hurting people, or the prospect of getting killed or incarcerated. He didn't care what people called him, he wouldn't do it. Once in a while, his friends of the Spaniard man's crew would go out and do a hold up and come back and bring him some dope because he was too drunk to go with them. The Spaniard loved Juan because he knew how smart and talented Juan was, and he also knew that when Juan got himself some dope, money, girls, a car, or whatever, he would always share, and would never, ever, drop a dime on anyone. It was surreal. Here was this crew of highly talented artists (the Spaniard was an awesome Flamenco guitarist and singer, and the owner of one of Juan's hideouts was a gifted poet and painter with a doctorate in literature). I guess you could consider their crimes part of their research for their art. But not all of Juan's friends were from academia and the art world.

Loco had been imprisoned for most of his adult life and was a champion boxer in prison. He had gotten released while Juan was living at Lolita's house. They quickly became partners in party and crime, and while Juan refused to do any violent crimes like Loco wanted, they did go on a few interesting trips.

Juan and Loco would take the bus to go to a street party and could not find a ride back to their place because the city buses had stopped running. Loco suggested they steal a car because he was tired of walking, a good suggestion, Juan thought, since he was tired too. Loco would tell Juan to watch out for trouble until he got the car unlocked. They would push it away from the parking space, so as to not make noise when the car started. They would then go home and pick up some money Juan had stashed away and go cop blow in their stolen car. When they were done driving around they would park the car in the bushes close to a building in their neighborhood and lock it so nobody would steal it from them. They would use the car for a few days and Loco would then sell it to someone in the underworld for cheap. If Juan or Loco needed to use it all they had to do was pop it open with their slim Jim and re hot wire it. Loco was the brother of one of Juan's prostitute friends, Lolita. She was dark skinned, good looking, had a couple of kids that she didn't care for, a bum of a husband, and she liked fucking almost as much as sucking on a crack pipe. Her house was the local go to spot to get high, hang out, crash, etc. Lolita had some contacts in the underworld and even had some pull with local politicians' sons; she screwed a couple of them, no one could resist her ass, even when she was strung out. Some of Juan's gay protégés would also crash there and Juan would protect them from any troubles. They wanted a piece of him but didn't say anything because they knew how crazy Juan could be. They preferred him as a friend. Juan had a reputation of starting fights everywhere he went (the local bars all had a picture of him where the bouncer was, warning them to not let Juan in) and beating the shit out of anybody who didn't pay him for services or dope, unless they were a woman or a really close friend like Enrique, Carlitos, Pepe, Joe, the Spaniard, the poet, or, of course, Lolita. Lolita's place started as a cool place to hang out and then turned into a full blown crack house. There were a couple of stick candles on the dinner table with ashes everywhere. The only way to get fire to smoke was to grab an old match and rub it against a glowing red stove burner until it produced a flame. It was almost painful for Juan to watch her destroy herself, but there was nothing he could do; he was doing the same.

Juan kept an apartment for himself and Enrique at the village, where they could hide out and crash. There was a mini refrigerator, a couple of fold out fabric pieces of furniture and a miniature metal oscillating fan that was so noisy he could not fall asleep unless he was wasted. They also kept rolling papers to smoke with. Juan kept a collection of empty liquor bottles in the kitchen. Among them was the bottle of Black Tower that he drank from the night he met the girl of his dreams. It was like a bottle of hope that some day he would get his shit together and marry her and have a family and live happily forever.

But the truth was heavy; he was going to hell on a speedboat unless he kicked his cocaine and alcohol habit. He just didn't know it yet, he thought he was just living life to the fullest and having fun. At the end of his street days he was in such a bad state that he had no place to sleep because he had sold the apartment with Enrique to go get high. Big mistake, you don't ever let go of your lair until you have another one. Years later, when Enrique died from aids pneumonia while kicking his heroin habit at the same treatment facility where Juan first got clean, Juan wished he had done things differently and perhaps save his most beloved friend, Enrique. Juan would never forget the phone call from Enrique's ex, Carmelita. She told him the sad news of Enrique's death. Juan called the rehab center right away and asked what happened. The lady told him that his friend had died in his sleep but that it was OK because Enrique had accepted Jesus as his savior and he went to heaven. Juan was furious that Enrique had not gotten the medical attention he needed and he knew that Enrique would have survived if they had just given him Suboxone or taken him to a hospital. Juan hated fanaticism and all the genocide it caused humanity. Juan had been clean for over a decade by then, and had also developed a deep hatred for religious practices that harmed humans.

Juan would never recover from not having been able to save his friend Enrique.

Enrique was 6'2" and his best talent was picking up women. My god, this guy was good! Juan had met Enrique outside of his favorite hangout in college town. Enrique came up to Juan and offered him a swig of "chichaíto", a mix of white rum and anisette. That started a friendship that would never ever falter. They kept talking and Enrique suggested that they go find some girls to party with, so they walked to the nearest payphone and finagled the operator to connect them to a party line for free. They ended up talking to a couple of girls that were having a party about thirty minutes away from them. They got in Enrique's car and went chasing after the tail. In the way, they kept drinking and smoking weed and never found the girls or the party, so they had to come back to college town. Juan had gotten too drunk, so they decided to go cop some coke to wake him up. It was too late though; by the time they made it to Beautiful, Enrique's favorite project, Juan was puking up a storm through the window and could not stop. Enrique had to carry Juan up the stairs to his apartment and lay him in bed. Those two had incredible stories together, sharing women, dope runs, weapons runs, parties, homelessness together, drinking all their money and panhandling for food, resorts, casinos, driving around the island just because they had two grand in their pocket, living like they had two million. Getting into fights in bars, running from the law, it was straight out of a movie. If only they had been able to stop on time, who knows?, maybe they would be partners in a successful business, they had the goods; guts and intelligence. My goodness!, what I would give for half of what they had, when they had it...

Enrique got himself arrested on some robbery charges and when he got out of prison, called Juan for some help. Juan had been clean and sober for a few years now, he owned a house, was married, and had a small auto repair business. Juan was so glad to hear from his old friend, they really loved each other those two. Enrique's girlfriend was going to pay for the plane ticket and Juan already had a place for him to crash until he got on his feet. Enrique was supposed to call back with his flight number but that would be the last time they ever spoke. Enrique died a few years later without Juan being able to help him. So sad, so, so sad. Juan will always love him, and will always remember how they used to tell people they were brothers, even though they weren't. Enrique taught Juan the audacity required to survive in the streets, the fierce appetite for love, and the bravery to expose your inner self, a requirement in order to cultivate deep relationships, especially with complete strangers. From Enrique Juan learned to take chances, many times without calculation, just for the experience, to fly with the wind just to see where you would end. He also taught him to secure a lair and some food, before anything else. He taught him to not hang out too much in the same place, so he could not be easily found. Enrique was a master of escape and could make some dope and wine appear just as easy as he could make female underwear disappear. He was a master manipulator, he would get women to buy him cars, pay for his rent, buy him clothes, get him jobs, you name it. Everybody loved him. He had that magnetism and charisma that very few people Juan met ever had. It was surreal, almost magic, to watch Enrique put people under his spell, and he wasn't even trying. Juan wanted that, but could only exert that type of power on few people. He understood it was a learned skill and it took a lot of honing, but it was achievable.

Another piece of work that was part of the crew was Carlitos. This was a real psycho dope fiend raised in the mountains surrounding the big city. He was a heavy equipment operator by trade, but his real skill was finding gay guys to turn a trick in the middle of nowhere. I mean, this guy could find a John on the dark side of the moon, no kidding, and walk out with money from that car in five minutes flat. "Come one Juan, we got us some money, lets go cop and go the city and party!" he would tell Juan as he came back to the plaza where Juan was waiting for him to come back. Carlitos would wear his pants really tight so that his oversized sack would protrude and attract more clients. If someone said something to him about it he would ask them what the fuck was it to them. You see, Carlitos had a very quick temper and would fight at the drop of a hat. He didn't care how big you were, it was on! And he could kick like a mule, yes sir! Sometimes Juan would wait until Carlitos got into a fight and find some unsuspecting soul to bet against Carlitos; easy money! Juan wasn't too shabby either when it came to fighting. He was wily and even though he always took a couple of punches, he would always end up on top of the other guy in the mounted position asking him to surrender. I think he even did it as a sport for a while. His friend Albert and him had girlfriends in the same public housing building and would go see them and meet after. They would go to the nearest bar and find a couple of guys and start a fight. Juan once started a fight that ended up with five guys trying to hit him and Albert wasn't even in the fight. Juan had thought that Albert had gotten jumped by a bunch of guys and Juan started punching all of them. Well, they went after Juan but he fought them off. When he got tired he asked them to make a line because he could only fight them one by one. And they did!!! Anyways, Juan's friends broke out the pistols and scared everybody away and the fight was over. Later on Albert asked Juan what the fuck was he doing, and they both started laughing when Albert told him he was never in the fight but that he enjoyed watching Juan fight. Lololol; fucking guys!

Juan had to change hangout spots for a while after that. Many stories started to surface on the street about Juan being killed, or Juan being jailed, or some other bullshit. He was hot and he knew it. Drugs and alcohol were taking a toll on his body and his street reputation, he didn't have the stamina or the strength he was used to and anybody could beat him in a fight. That was not good. It was the beginning of the end of his street days, but not for long. He still had another run in him. I guess Juan wanted to live forever and do as he pleased, good or bad. A lot of his friends had started to settle down, get imprisoned or died off. Some, like his Dominican friend Serge, managed to sporadically binge and party but they always managed to keep rolling and bounce back. Little David got himself a job with the power company, got married and would go on binges once in a while, maybe get kicked out of his house for a little and come back. Little David, Serge and Juan would buy flowers and bundle them up in plastic wrap and sell them at stoplights in neighboring towns. They would do OK, but would party all their money away. On mother's day and Valentine's they would make good money and would piss it all away on drugs, booze and the casinos. They all eventually parted ways but Juan was stuck and he knew it. There was no denying it, Juan had some fun for some time. But the time had come to grow up or something like that. I guess Juan knew how short life was and he didn't want to miss anything. It was hard to stop trying to find a good party or a good time. All he wanted to do was have lots of fun without any headaches or having to answer to anybody. He wished he could get paid for partying or destroying himself, which is what he was doing. I guess one of the main lures of his lifestyle was his ability to up and go whenever he wanted. All he needed was money, but not to serve it, only to serve him. He looked at the people who had responsibilities as cattle in a fence, as slaves to a machine that produced more slaves. The family who slaved over to pay their bills so they could indoctrinate their children on the art of serving the slave making machine with joy. He saw something obscene in that. It was sacrilege to the spirit of humanity, he thought. Of course he manipulated this very truthful thought to continue down the road of destruction, but he had a point. Many years later, Juan still felt different than the rest of the world, even after getting clean, but he was kind of OK with it. He still raged against the slave making machine but tried to share his thoughts in a manner that could free some souls from the blood fields that the machine fed on.

JUAN ALMOST GETS KILLED

Sometime after Juan had sold off his apartment with Enrique at the Pan-American village he returned with his friend Pepito to visit some friends. Pepito was an Army vet with a taste for cocaine and beer. He drove an old Oldsmobile and liked to go on binges once in a blue moon. He worked at the Veterans hospital in the island and had a cute girlfriend that he constantly fought with. On this occasion Pepito and Juan had been partying for about 24 hours or so and wanted some female company. Juan went to his friend's house, she was bi-sexual and lived with her girlfriend. They talked a little and then decided to go to the town to drink some more. When they returned to the apartment all their furniture had been stolen. They quickly found out who had done it and Juan decided to go to the neighboring project to look for the guy. It turned out that the guy was the brother of the local drug lord and had a nasty heroin and cocaine habit. Juan and his two girlfriends caught up with the guy by the stairs on the east side of the building. When Nereida saw the guy she threw a cup of ice to his face and the guy punched her. When Juan saw this, he immediately jumped the guy and he punched him on the face which made him fall to the ground. But this guy came back up like it was some type of horror movie. He was so tweaked on whatever he was that he did not feel the impact and started fighting Juan. Juan punched him again and the guy fell and came back up like a movie zombie! That's when Juan decided to pull out his box cutter knife and cut the guy. Thank God the guy took off running when he saw the knife and Juan could not catch up with him. Many years later Juan is still grateful that he did not catch him with the swing of his knife, just the thought of having tried to kill another human made Juan very sad. Juan started calling for his friend to come down so they could leave. He knew this guy would come back with his brother and that meant guns and trigger happy drug lords and retaliation for Juan having tried to kill the guy's brother. Juan was in the car waiting for his friend to come down the stairs when the guy that ran comes back with a bat in his hands. He was coming from the passenger side and his brother from the driver's side. Juan was in the driver's seat when the guy starts smashing the windows with the bat. At the same time his brother starts to pull a Tech 9 sub machine gun out of his pants to shoot Juan with. Juan tells the guy to not kill him and at that same moment the girls get in between the machine gun and Juan. That's when Juan saw the opportunity and ran as fast as he could out of the parking lot. He went in a ditch that some heavy equipment operators were digging to get out of the line of fire, he must have put about fifty yards between him and the shooter. The workers jumped out of their machines and ran for cover when they saw the gunman chasing Juan. Juan crossed the busy intersection so fast that it seemed surreal. On the other side of it was a police station and Juan took refuge in it. The place doubled as a gym and the gunman did not dare go after him. A little later the girls arrived and told the cops what had happened. Juan ended up being escorted back to the project where his cousin was the man and where he would be safe. This was one of about three times where Juan got into very dangerous situations as a consequence of living the fast life. The scare did not last long, he was back running the streets that same night. It's like he had a secret death wish. It would not be the last time Juan almost got killed.

JUAN'S COUSIN, WOW BOY

One of Juan's relatives was a cop who had had an affair with a woman from the projects where he worked as director of the police athletic league. She had a son from him and he was happy with his little boy. From the time he was little Wow boy excelled in sports and leadership but the only opportunities for money and fame in the projects were related to vice. Wow's stepdad was a ranking member of the local drug dealing ring and showed him all the ins and outs of the business. By the time Wow was in his late teens he had his own retail marihuana operation and all the gold jewelry to go along with it. Juan had not seen Wow for a long time. When he went back to Puerto Rico in 1987, he had convinced one of his childhood friends, Joey, to register for college with him. Joey had a reputation for liking to smoke weed and once in a while do some cocaine. He eventually convinced Juan to try cocaine. Juan never blamed him for it, though, he would have tried it anyways. He was in love the minute he tried it. Joey had met Wow without Juan introducing them. Eventually Joey reunited Wow and Juan and they rekindled their ties. When Juan went to the project to visit Wow for the second time, they went to see a friend of Wow to introduce to them. While standing in front of the guy's house, a shooting started very close to where Juan was. He went into the guy's house for protection until the shooting stopped. The local gunmen had started shooting at Wow's brother's balcony to mess with him. Wow's brother, Blackie, grabbed his magnum and shot back at the shooters. It had all been a birthday prank on Blackie. The shooters were all his friends. That's the way these people pulled pranks on each other. Juan was shocked at first but got used to the lifestyle of the projects. He would go to play basketball whenever he was not in school. He started getting five dollar bags from his cousin and selling them for fifteen or twenty at the university. Sometimes he would stay with his cousin and help him bag the coke. They would all have pistols on them. Wow had a big mirror that he used to put the cocaine on. He would then mix it with lactose and bag it. If the coke was a little humid, he would use a hairdryer to blow under the mirror and dry it. He would not bag the coke if it was cloudy either, because it made the coke damp and people would not be able to snort it. To test the quality of the coke, Juan would call one of the local mainline junkies and give him a five dollar bag to test. They would come back in a little while and tell Wow if it was good. Sometimes wow would put too much lactose in the mix and it would decrease the potency of the drug too much. He would then have to empty all the bags and add more pure cocaine.

Wow boy got most the services he needed by paying with cocaine instead of cash. Haircuts, work on his car, ironing of his clothes, even sex, he paid for them with dope. He would buy guns from the local police and pay them with coke. At any one time Wow boy would have four or five cars that he alternated using so as to not be predictable.

He would also have lookouts all around the area of the project where he operated and would never keep any dope on him. For that he had different safe houses. Juan and Wow would lose contact for a while when Juan hit his bottom but Juan would visit him a couple of more times after he got out of rehab. Many years later Juan spoke with Wow boy on the phone and Wow was working a regular job and running a bodyguard service to support his children. They were glad to talk and Juan would stay in contact with him from time to time. Wow boy visited Juan a couple of times and would hire Wow boy and his crew whenever he wanted to come to the island. Juan did not need protection, he just wanted to hang out with the old crew and his cousin. They had all gotten out of the dope business, gotten training in security and weapons tactics, and were now the baddest clandestine personal security team in the island with a license. They were all experts in street fighting techniques. All of them still lived in the projects part time, even though those were not their main residences. Not even cops would fuck with them because they knew that these guys were walking a straight line and could also provide security in places where a low profile was needed and the cops did not dare enter without a 100 people for backup. All the information on clients was kept completely confidential and they never, ever turned on each other. They would spill their last drop of blood defending the other, their families, and their clients. Wow boy still kept his "Santeria" collars and religion for protection, and would always sponsor new recruits into this two million year old religion. I went to meet Wow boy one time and almost got killed by his son. You cant' just walk into a project in Puerto Rico without proper company. It took a couple of phone calls and about two hours of waiting while sitting on a concrete bench by the basketball court before my identity was confirmed and I was allowed to meet with Wow boy for a cup of coffee. He put Juan on the phone for a proper ass chewing and then he proceeded to introduce me to all his kids, grandmother, mother, brothers and some of the people in his crew. Of course everybody in his crew wore ski masks and AK-47's, but they were glad to hang out with a friend of Juan. It was scary, I tell you, but after a few minutes it was like being part of the family. They fed me until I could not breathe and showed me pictures of all their mistresses and wives just to make sure I didn't run into them and tried to pick them up. These fucking guys are awesome! They took me to one of their private clubs by a beach on the south side of the island. They blindfolded me for the last hour of the trip and made sure I didn't have any electronic devices on me before I got in the car. You had to drive into a cave at low tide because the road got covered by the sea when the tide came up. Inside the cave system they had a bar, sleeping quarters for about twenty people, a little self serve restaurant, music equipment, radio equipment, etc. They cooked and we all ate, and drank and played war video games, and swam in the ocean with beautiful women that accompanied us, and exchanged stories until everybody was tired. We all stayed there until the next day and returned to the northern part of the island, where they dropped me off at my hotel without me ever having let them know where I was staying. These guys were good, very good. They handed me a card that was transparent and looked like it had a chip inside and told me to press it if I ever needed help, they would contact me. Wow boy thanked me for coming to visit him and told me to look out for Juan, he was part of the crew forever....

JUAN'S LITTLE SECRET

Juan had many talents, he was gorgeous, bi-lingual, super smart, well educated, and well equipped in the hydraulics department. He had about eight inches of love, and he did not know that was above average, so he threw that thing like there was no tomorrow. Women could not get enough of him. Maybe that was why he caught every damn cuddi in the island; gono, crabs, etc. He even caught herpes for not protecting himself. Thank God he didn't catch HIV, it was a miracle. I mean, he protected himself back in the days of prostitution, but he didn't do so with most women. It was really a dumb luck thing. Juan's favorite position was the missionary because he could see the woman's facial responses to his work. He gave himself completely when he had sex with his women, he was a very passionate man, very sexual. Some of his friends suggested he let women stick their fingers in his butt because it would make him come harder, but Juan wanted nothing to do with shit in the bedroom, not even when he got paid, unless he got paid extra to stick his willie in a butt. To each his own he thought, but it was not for him. Juan's friends sometimes told him that he might be bi-sexual but he disagreed, Juan only put his thingy in gay men's mouths for money, that's it, he hated every second of it. He did not hate gay people though, on the contrary, he really admired their bravery to stand up to a society who was outright violent towards them. He admired their work ethic, their dedication, and above all, their honesty. They also had the best music in their clubs, and in many occasions harbored him when he was on the run. One of his best gay friends was Luisito, a critical care nurse in the trauma center of the island. This man was an angel. He took Juan in from the street, gave him a place to sleep, fed him, and never asked for sex, a penny or nothing. Juan stayed with him for a while but eventually had to go. You see, this humongous coke habit of Juan made him stab Luisito in the back. One night Juan came home and Luisito was not there. Juan was jonesing for some more coke but had no money, so he decided to take Luisito's TV, VCR, and Polaroid camera and sell them to the dope dealer. Juan really messed up this time. He had bitten the hand that fed him. Juan went into hiding after that because he could not face Luisito. After Juan had gotten out of rehab he went and relapsed and ran into Luisito. He apologized but Luisito did not care, he was a true friend and even took Juan in again and gave him some money. It turned out that Luisito had been lovers with little David for some time and Luisito was still in love with little David(one of Juan's best friends). By some turn of events they started talking and Juan figured out who Luisito was talking about. They found little David and hung out and partied some. Luisito was not into drugs, he just liked his beer and once in a blue moon would smoke a little weed. Juan would never forget him. Many years later Juan would still think of Luisito and wish he could pay him back for all his kindness.

JUAN GOES TO REHAB

Juan had decided to get help with his substance abuse problems after being confronted by his auntie. She got him to agree to get help. They found a place in the southern part of the island where they would take him in. It was the former brothel for Isabel Oppenheimer, or Isabel "la negra". In its heyday this brothel was the best of the best, it even had a contract with the US Navy to service their boys during world war II and military exercises in the island. Where the bar used to be now existed an altar to preach to impoverished addicted souls. It had been converted into a drug rehab facility. The owner was a retired junkie who had gotten clean through religion. Their system was based on Pentecostal religious fanatical beliefs, but Juan didn't care, he just wanted some relief from the hurting the drugs and alcohol had put on him. He didn't know what to expect when he got there, but he hoped it would be a place where he could get better. Juan honestly thought they were going to fix him so he could drink and snort socially, without hitting the crack pipe or ending homeless, you know, like normal people. He figured he would be here for a little while and then move on. The first few weeks were a little rough. He had a bunk bed in a room with another five people. Most of them were kicking heroin and were sent there from prisons around the island. Some of them would bring stashes of cigarettes and drugs into the center when they were transported there from prison. Many could not stay clean in prison because there were more drugs inside than outside. Sometimes half of the inmate population in the island would test positive for heroin. They had cell phones and guns inside the prison! They made their own alcoholic beverage called "múscula", which was like hooch. It was not Black Label but it performed beautifully. Most of these guys were veterans at being dope fiends and were accustomed to all the career benefits. They also possessed something that Juan envied; unbreakable hope of a better day ahead.

Juan was withdrawing from cocaine and alcohol abuse. The physical symptoms were quite different but the psychological torture was equally painful. Juan developed a severe flu that had him down for a good week. He was coughing up stuff like he had never seen before. Juan used to smoke cocaine out of ash pipes he made from aluminum cans he found on the street. He didn't carry paraphernalia on him for fear of getting caught with anything on him. The ash had gotten on his lungs, along with the resin from all the marihuana he smoked, and was now coming out in chunks of black and green mucus. He also developed a monster lower back ache that would not quit. All he wanted to do was sleep. His body was recovering from all the punishment. Little by little he started to feel better physically but his brain was asking for some dope and alcohol. Juan rode this wild horse by getting immersed in the chores of living in a poor man's Betty Ford center. The building where he stayed did not have a bathroom or running water. You had to go outside to a free standing outhouse with a toilet in it and the showers were in a separate building covered with a metal roof. It was a country setting. Through individual donations the owner had built two quasi modern dormitories with running water and bathrooms inside. Juan guessed there were 100 clients living in the center on any given day. He woke up every morning and went to the morning church service, had breakfast, and went back to his dorm to read the bible and talk to his roommates. They all had stories about their families, prison, their crimes, violence, death, money, and poverty. The HIV incidence was very high amongst the clients, and a lot of them were only taking AZT, Ensure and Diflucan because the cocktails were not available yet, it was 1993; the year when the cocktails had just started getting tested and were not available in his island yet. Juan always had a soft spot for people that were sick, he was a natural champion and protector. He was always sharing the candy that his grandmother sent him via mail. Candy helped heroin addicts go through their hellatious withdrawal ordeal. Eventually Juan became the head of the heroin detox unit in the center. The detox methods were brutal and Spartan. The clients would come in after they had dosed in the street that morning and would go through the paperwork session while they were still nodding. By the next morning they were in full withdrawal. Their arms and legs would flail uncontrollably up in the air, with chills and vomiting setting by the end of the second night. By the second day, they would be laying in bed hallucinating and picking up imaginary hard candy from the floor, unwrapping it and eating it. Apparently the mixture of heroin with horse tranquilizer that they were putting in street junk was causing even worse withdrawal symptoms than normal. Juan had to stay awake every night to hold them to make sure they would not fall or hit their heads against the metal framed beds. He had to take them to the toilet and shower because they could not hold themselves up. Some of them would go in the shower and masturbate repeatedly to alleviate the withdrawal symptoms. They said it was the only thing that helped. Everybody kicked cold turkey, no sedatives, no doctor, just a prayer and a deal with God to accept Jesus as their savior. The owners of the center figured that if they died, they would at least go to heaven. This appeased their conscience, if they had any, and society did not care. Juan did not understand that they did not know any better; they really thought they were doing the best they could. There was no Suboxone available those days and physician assisted withdrawal was only for rich people or those with health insurance. After all, these were street junkies, ex-cons, the throwaways of the island, the lepers of the world, as Juan called them. This always bothered Juan because he felt deep love for his humans, specially the throwaways. After a while, Juan started to forget about his life and got immersed in the daily activities of the center. He was basically an unpaid employee doing the dirty work, but he liked being able to save lives. Besides, Juan later understood that these humans shared something in common with him; they were survivors of a war that had claimed the lives of tens of thousands of his countrymen and women per year, for well over a decade. These were the maimed souls of humanity's scourge; genocidal class-ism.

There were two counselors in the center, one was a soft handed pastor that Juan adored and that had never been an addict, and the other one was a street savvy ex-junkie and ex-con who had become a pastor and turned his life around. The director was also the owner and a reformed junkie. His wife and daughter ran the office and all the administrative duties.

Juan accepted Jesus as his savior and jumped into the religious fanatic world with both feet. He figured that was what everybody needed to do, and since they said that God would cast out the demons of addiction, lust, and other garden variety demons, it all made sense to him. He spent a lot of time reading the bible, shoot, he read the whole thing and even started preaching and teaching it. There were some things he did not like though. Masturbating was a sin, so he held it as long as he could and then, when he couldn't hold it any longer, he did it and asked for forgiveness from God. This really fucked with Juan; if God made me, then why is a natural desire a sin? That would make God the maker of sin. It also bothered him to read Paul and his hateful speeches in Romans, where he went off on people for being who they were. Juan had a lot of gay friends and he didn't like the fact that Paul sent them all to hell. Years later Juan understood that the bible was just a group of books (originating from "biblos" in Greek) that had been put together in a larger book, by a bunch of men with serious control issues, during the council of Niece. It was all man made and Paul did not even meet Jesus. He was in the bible to try to gain the favor of the former Habiru, even though the Hebrews will deny having ever been Habiru, who knows, thought Juan?, maybe they weren't, Juan was not an expert anyways. As a matter of fact, Juan had serious doubts that Jesus would have even associated with somebody as self righteous as Paul, not because he had been a mass murderer of Christians, but because he continued to let his self righteousness lead him to the condemnation of others. Juan had to go through a lot of emotional pain to arrive at this conclusion and it would come many years after his stint in rehab.

Juan continued to work in the center as a leader and then took the responsibility of leading the sales team. Every Saturday a group of clients from the center would get in a couple of vans and go to all the barrios in the area to sell fundraiser candy door to door. It was a way for the clients to contribute to the center and to get slowly back into society. It was dangerous though; some of the guys were hot in the street and Juan had to send them to different towns. A failure in logistics by Juan could prove deadly for his friends. There was also the danger of the guys using the money from their sales to go buy drugs, which happened on several occasions. Juan developed an enormous love for all these humans who were considered throwaways. They had so much love inside of them, even after being kicked and robbed of their dignity, and so many years behind prison walls. Even while being ravaged by the scorn of AIDS they kept their heads up high and hoped for a better tomorrow and a hug from their children and wives. Juan could see the light of love shine on their faces when their families came to see them on Sundays. You couldn't even tell they had nothing to their name, or that they had all the odds stacked up against them, or that they had been hard core dope fiends. For those few hours with their families the air smelled sweet, there was peace in their souls, and you would swear that evil was just a story they told in Hollywood movies. Funny, Juan thought, how humans can turn into magicians who make spirits and flowers bloom in the air, with nothing more than a true promise and a smile of the soul. But they also had a dark side. They would turn violent in a heartbeat if they felt they were being threatened. The leaders of the center had to do searches routinely. They would find a ton of homemade weapons and dispose of them. If the power went out on the center the leaders had flashlights to guide their way in the darkness. The problem was that some of the clients did not like authority and would throw stones at the flashlights hoping to hit the leaders. It was pretty brutal and a lot of the guys found it funny. Nevertheless Juan made some deep friendships in rehab. There was the musician-painter-chef that wrote the music score for Juan's Christian songs. Juan had a good voice and Joey helped him develop it. Pretty soon they were traveling the island as a music group representing the center. It was nice to get out and travel throughout the island. Juan never forgot those days. He was at peace and felt useful and wanted. It did not matter to him that he was living in a rehab facility with a bunch of other guys with rap sheets from here to Hong Kong, or that he had to share a shower and toilets with other people. He felt safe, believe it or not. Just the fact that he was clean was soothing to him. It helped that he didn't have to hustle to keep a roof or food, or dope. That helped. Another good friend Juan made was Joshua. He was a retired boxer who had shot dope for most of his adult life. He was about 6'3" and 220 and in his late forties. He made a living as a cab driver in New York for many years and had married an excellent woman from the Dominican Republic and had a son in his mid twenties. Joshua's dope habit and his constant womanizing had strained the relationship with his wife but she always loved him. On Saturdays Joshua and Juan would go to his wife's house and she would give them lunch. Joshua called himself the terror of all married men in the neighborhood. He always ended up dating married women and in a couple of occasions almost got killed by their husbands. Joshua had a quick temper and was not scared of anybody. One time his son's neighbor went to his house and slapped his son over some disagreement. When Joshua found out he went straight to the neighbor's house and beat the shit out of him, no questions asked. Joshua had been a boxer and a trainer and had the balls to fight King Kong if he fucked with him or his loved ones, period! But inside that toughness there was also a delicate soul, capable of empathizing with the pain of his fellow human. Juan remembers his first new year's eve in the center. The emotions were running deep inside of him. Juan really missed his mother, who had been dead for 14 years, he remembered his family, the one he had isolated himself from so as not to embarrass them with his constant drunkenness and drugged state, he remembered his beloved Lucía, the one that he fell in love with. He remembered his innocence before it was lost to the fire of the hell he had lived as a consequence of addiction. He remembered his aunt and his grandmother. How much he wished he had chosen a different path and not lost control. How much he longed to be a normal person, and not have this monster inside of him, the one who made him sacrifice his soul at the altar of pain. In the middle of the hope of being able to have a clean new year's eve, he felt the fear of never being able to be loved unconditionally again. Right there, at that moment, Joshua came over to Juan and, like a father, hugged him and let Juan's sobbing empty on his chest. Juan would never forget such a gesture of profound empathy and strength. Many years later, while Juan was divorcing from Joshua's Niece, he learned of Joshua's death in a recliner inside a hospital room. Hepatitis-c had given Joshua's liver all it could handle and Joshua fell asleep while hepatomegaly and hepatic encephalopathy finished him off. He was a good friend and I don't think he was scared of death like Juan. Maybe it was because Joshua's father was a pastor and had indoctrinated him about living forever, and that was ingrained in his psyche. Who knows? Juan really loved him and he loved Juan. So many good people were trapped in the empty holes of their own souls. Juan knew there would always be business for this rehab center as long as there were Joshuas and Juans in the world.

Life in this rehab center was kind of another world. Even though Juan would eventually sever ties with organized religion, he always kept a special place in his heart for that place. It was his first encounter with hope and the brutal path that is sometimes taken to reach it.

During one of Juan's passes to his grandmother's house, he ran into one of the bar owners on the University strip where he did most of his hanging. The bar owner had forbidden Juan to come into his place because Juan had beaten one of the patrons of the bar up over a cocaine debt. It had been about nine months since Juan got clean and he decided to walk by the neighborhood. Rafo told Juan that some of his friends had gotten locked up over some counterfeit money and even insinuated that Juan had ratted them out and gotten away. That pissed Juan off but he did not let it show. One of the guys that got nabbed was a good friend of Juan and Juan was not a snitch, never! He told Rafo that he went to rehab and that he had nothing to do with whatever had happened. Juan wished he could talk to the guys and tell them that he had nothing to do with what happened, but he had no way of finding out where they were and did not know their real names, only their street aliases. One of them was a cook, the other a construction worker, and the other was a Dominican part-time junkie, who did odd jobs and was always trying to make counterfeit money to distribute. He and Juan had gotten high together a few times but Juan did not like to hang out with people who mainlined, he never knew if they were going to overdose and become a liability. Juan had enough problems keeping himself alive. It did make for an exciting time; all the copping and watching someone play Russian roulette with a hypodermic, all the ritual of prepping the drug and messing with veins. Juan could tell that about half of the vice came from the ritual. The Dominican guy was also bi-sexual but he never tried to mess with Juan, he just kept trying to get Juan to move some fake money for him. Juan went with him a couple of times to try to buy stuff in Dominican bars that were poorly lit and it worked for a couple of times, then a couple of the bartenders noticed and refused to take the bills. They were of shitty quality. The only risk they ran was getting kicked out of the bars because they knew they would not call the police; most of these people were illegal anyway and the bars were just fronts for prostitution. The always had female bartenders who doubled as hookers. You had to buy them a drink first, which was usually diluted wine, then they would offer to dance with you in a room with a veil at the entrance. In the room you could grab their ass and feel them all you wanted. If you got hot, you could take them upstairs for a piece and a price, usually forty bucks for them and eighteen for the room manager. It was an assembly line. Good pussy too, according to Juan. Back to the Dominican though. The funny thing is that to this day Juan wonders what happened to his friends. In a way he wishes he could straighten out the facts with them. Now that Juan had a life and a family it would be stupid to run into this people and them think he had something to do with their incarceration and end up killing him or hurting him for no good reason at all. Rumors kill people in the street every day, more than overdoses! Juan did run into one of the guys from the crew at a 12 step program convention. Juan hugged him but the guy was really skittish towards Juan. Juan did not really pay much attention at the lack of warmth in the guy and kept going. In one occasion Juan saw the Dominican drive by the strip after Juan had relapsed a few months after he got out of rehab. He just drove by and smiled. Many years later Juan still was a little weary of running into his friends that got locked up over the counterfeit money, but there was nothing he could do about the lies people said back then. He knew the truth and that is all that mattered.

JUAN GETS MARRIED

Juan and his girlfriend were both sitting there eating ice cream. He had gotten out of rehab and enrolled in classes at the local university. He was also making a couple of extra dollars selling advertising for one of his college professors. Life was OK for Juan, but he still felt lonely. Loneliness had been Juan's faithful companion ever since his mother died. It never left him by himself. He could not explain it, even to this day I think he dances with her. He feels it a curse sometimes, and sometimes a blessing. Juan had met his girlfriend while he was in rehab. Her aunt's husband was in rehab with Juan and drove the van that transported the clients around. They had become great friends and on Saturdays they would go have lunch at his wife's house. Juan and Judy became friends and later started dating when Juan left rehab. It was nothing serious at the time but Juan kept seeing her. Juan had had a slip and gotten drunk and did some coke a couple of months after leaving rehab. He also had started seeing a woman he knew from before. She was a really hot blooded girl with tremendous talent in the sack but he didn't think of her as relationship material. There was also another woman that he saw after rehab. This was an English teacher he was dating when he had been at the end of his run on the streets. She was a good person with almost as many issues as Juan, but had good intentions for Juan. Juan will never forget her boobs; he tells me those things were gorgeous and big!

She would do anything for him. She went crazy looking for Juan when he went to rehab and even though she begged his family to tell them where he was so she could visit him, his family didn't budge. He eventually found her after leaving rehab and bagged her one more time before he got married. Her boyfriend was at work and she got what she wanted. Juan never saw her again but still remembers her with affection. She was there for him when he really had nobody to lean on.

To tell you the truth, I think Juan got married just because it didn't seem like a threatening thing. All these other women seemed threatening to Juan, like they would stab him on the back if the shit hit the fan. You see, Juan had agreed to marry his wife because she would not move in with him. He had also gotten her infected with an incurable std that doesn't kill. She didn't budge, she stood by him. That impressed Juan and he proceeded to marry her. On hindsight, she was the best woman a man could want by his side, but Juan should not have married her. He should have waited to fall in love, he should have looked for Lucía, the true love of his life. He should have never abused drugs, my God!, so many things he should have not done. But if my uncle had tits, he would be my aunt... Juan eventually went after Lucía and divorced Judy. Judy remarried and had a couple of kids. Her husband was a great guy and they were very happy together. Juan lost contact with her but would sporadically run into her when he lived in Florida. Juan never had any regrets about divorcing Judy, it was the right thing to do because it gave Judy a chance to find someone who was in love with her and would make her happy.

JUAN GOES TO JAIL

Juan and his wife had split after less than a year of marriage because he had gone back to drinking and drugging and turned their lives into a hellhole. Juan did not know about the need for people with addiction disorders to get continued treatment. He thought that the people who prayed for him at the center had cast out the addiction demons and he was good to go. That meant he could drink normally because Jesus turned water into wine. As long as he didn't do drugs, he was OK, right? Well, three bottles of wine, three months of no positive reinforcement, and one pissed off formerly sleeping gorilla later, Juan was running to find a ride to the project to cop some coke.

If he had known the shit storm that was about to hit him, he would not have done it. Poor Juan, poor boy, poor lonely boy who just needed his momma, that's all he needed. He got tore up the first time and most every time he drank after that. He tried to control it, with little success. His fiancée found out about it but she still married him. It was not going to last long. After she left him and signed up for the air force to get away from him, Juan went to live with his biological father in the US for a little. It was not long before he got drunk and high again and things were not working out with his father, they never did. Juan started dating an old flame and before he knew it he had moved in with her. It was pretty cool at the beginning, lots of sex and partying. But then it started to go south, it had to. Juan was drinking again and found a connection for coke. Now both he and his girlfriend were doing it. Problems with money arose and Juan really just wanted out of there. One night he got into an argument with this woman over some money he had given her to hold. She refused to give him the money so Juan started to look for it in her purse and when he turned around she had a glass vase to hit him with. Juan reacted quickly and grabbed the hand that she had the vase in and wrestled it away from her so as not to get his head cracked open. He then turned around to put the vase away from her, and when he turned to her she had another object in her hands to hit him with. This time Juan took the other object from her hands and grabbed her by the arm and pushed her against the bathroom wall with his fist raised. He told her to stop trying to hurt him and that he was leaving, she could keep the money. Juan started to pack a few things and the woman went to the phone, called 911 and told them that her boyfriend had beat her up and was stealing her car. Juan had bought a car on installments and sent the last payment with this woman and she kept the last receipt. Juan asked her what the hell she was talking about on the phone to the police. He just got in the car and took off. The woman told the cops that she was pregnant, that Juan had beat her up, even though he hadn't, and that he had stolen her car. Lo and behold, they believed her, maybe because she was white and Juan was Latino, who knows? So Juan turned himself in that same night and finds out he is being charged with aggravated battery, grand larceny auto, and who knows what else. The booked him at the county jail. The place was loud, Juan almost felt like he was inside some carnival ride where the stars were black and Hispanic people, dressed in blue overalls. It was weird though, all these people just acted like they were hanging out at the park; joking around, talking loud, laughing, and just hanging out like nothing was wrong, they were at home, it felt like. That was scary to Juan, when a person whose freedom has been taken away acts like they are at home; he didn't understand it. He would later understand that it is called doing time, not letting the time do you. Juan learned later that you never, ever, give your incarcerator the pleasure of seeing you suffer, NEVER!

The guards took Juan into a cell with two other inmates. There was a bunk bed on each side and a toilet right in front of everybody. Inmates were allowed only two flushes per hour and one bath every three days. That first night Juan did not sleep much and turned down the bologna sandwich that they offered him for a meal. The next day Juan got served with a restraining order, taken for a shower and moved to a cell with about twenty other inmates. That's when it finally hit Juan, he was in jail!, he felt the world crashing on him. All his stupid decisions had brought him here. He had not done what he was accused of but it didn't matter. He really, really wished he had listened to advice and had not fucked up his life with drugs, bad decisions and bad company. As he lay on the top bunk he could not contain his grief and pulled the thin covers over his head and started to sob. He will never forget what a black inmate did for him at that moment. This gentleman came over and saw his grief and right before he pulled the covers over his head, gave him a pat on his back and told Juan that it was going to be OK. Juan never saw the man again, even when he woke up. Maybe he was an angel. Juan went for his first appearance in front of a TV with a judge in it. It was like an assembly line, next, next, next. No humanity or what happened or nothing. People in jail are guilty unless they can afford to prove otherwise. They took Juan to a bigger cell where there were more people. Juan spent seven days in jail and then got bonded out. The same day he was about to be released the woman came to see him and to apologize for having put him in jail. They spent the night together and fucked like rabbits in the Discovery channel, so much for being in fear of Juan! The next day Juan had to leave because the woman's ex was coming back from work. She promptly had moved her ex back in after Juan went to jail. It was almost comical, she had removed Juan's pictures from the walls and put her ex's on. Juan had packed his bags that were still in the woman's house, Jezebel was her name. Juan took off in his car and went driving around looking to get high or drunk. He was lost, confused, pissed. What was he going to do? He had these charges on him and his life was a mess. He couldn't stay at his father's and he didn't know anybody. He couldn't leave the country until he was done with this case. He went to a bar and got drunk and just kept driving. He ran out of gas somewhere and just parked on the side of the road. He had been driving all night long trying to figure out what to do. Next morning two cops woke him up and told him he had to move the car but that he could not drive it or he would be arrested because he still smelled like alcohol. So Juan called his father and he came and got him to take the car back to Jezebel because she said she wanted it back. Juan had contacted his stepfather to see if he would pay for a hotel room and he did. Juan ended up knocking on his father's door after spending the night at the hotel. His father didn't want him there so he sent him to stay with a friend of his who owned a dealership. Juan started to work for this greedy Cuban guy who paid him 35 dollars a day and let him stay at his house. He kept drinking because he didn't want to feel the reality, it was too painful. He wanted to kill himself one night by cutting his wrists but when he started it was too painful, so he called his adoptive parents in Texas. Poor people, poor Juan, with all that pain and loneliness again. It was an empty feeling, like a big chunk of ice inside the heart, with a hole in the middle where 100 mph winds were going through. They cried with him on the phone, they soothed him and begged him not to do it. They prayed on the phone with him. Juan contacted a treatment center and went in. Right in the parking lot he downed three wine coolers to settle his nerves. They took him because his wife still had him under her insurance with the air force since they weren't divorced yet. He had called her and explained the situation to her and she helped him. She was a good woman. Juan spent 10 days in there and his father had arranged for Juan to go stay with a cousin of his by Florida's east coast. Juan hated the fact that his father didn't want to deal with him, as usual, dumping him on others, but he was grown up now and had to take care of himself, although he really needed someone to go to bat for him at this moment in his life. That had been another one of Juan's frustrations or character defects if you will. He didn't want the people that offered to bat for him, he wanted the ones who didn't want to bat for him!

At his cousin's Juan started to learn to work on cars and he liked it. He also started attending 12 step meetings and liked those too. He didn't feel at home but at least there were people there with similar problems. While staying at his cousin's Juan got visited by Jezebel and they hung out for a while. Everything seemed OK, she was going to drop the charges and Juan was going to move on with his life. The problem began when Juan told Jezebel that he was getting back with his wife. Big mistake! Jezebel took a letter that Juan had written to her, to the state attorney and they revoked his bond without Juan's knowledge. Juan had to move to his other cousin's house, where he started a job and got his own apartment. In the meantime, he had gone up to see his wife graduate from basic training and spent a weekend with her and they rekindled their relationship. They started planning to get back together when Juan was done with the case. It was not to be right away though. In Juan's visit to his case worker at the Jail complex a cop shows up and arrests Juan for violation of a restraining order. On the way to the jail the cop kept asking Juan if this was going to mess up his day, like he wanted to know that he was hurting him. It was like the cop was getting off on it. It was sickening for Juan to see that. This time Juan knew he was fucked. He was going to be in there for a long time without a bond. Juan had met with his public pretender for about fifteen minutes and he told him that they had no case and not to worry. This lawyer was cocky and full of himself. By the time they went in front of the Judge for trial, Jezebel was asking for the death penalty for Juan's crime of going back to his wife and letting her steal Juan's car with the help of the police. Justice for all! The lawyer comes over to Juan all nervous and informs him that the accuser wants his head on a platter. Juan stands there and listens to this attorney offer him a year in jail and goes on to tell Juan to take the plea bargain because he will be sent to a work release program where he can go home after he behaves good for a couple of weeks. Juan proceeded to tell the judge that Lucky Luciano had gotten a better deal than this. He signed the plea agreement not knowing what the consequences of being a convicted felon were. He had no idea he would not be able to get a job, rent a house, vote, nothing, he knew nothing. A couple of weeks go by and the work release guy comes in to interview Juan and informs him that work release programs don't take violent offenses. That really pissed off Juan and the Jaguar inside his soul woke up with a fight in his eyes. He wrote the judge about what had happened but the judge dismissed his letter and told him to contact his public defender, so he did. When the public pretender's letter came back it was full of insults from the pretender, so Juan sent the letter to the judge and the judge threw aside the conviction, reopened the case and assigned him a private lawyer. There was hope, Juan thought. At last someone seemed to see what was going on. It would be a long road to redemption though, Juan had just opened a distant door within a maze. It would take countless hours in the law library and long talks with old convicts to try to figure out a strategy to exit this university of crime.

There was so much wasted talent in jail, that Juan could not believe it. There was the artist who would paint gruesome street scenes on paper. Like the one of the black crack prostitute sucking on a Coke can crack pipe, with smoke coming out of the side of it, and a baby skeleton on a pool of blood that she had just given birth to. The artist would make a living in jail by drawing on postal envelopes that the inmates would send to their loved ones. It cost two racks of cookies for one of the artist's decorated envelopes. He really had talent. There was the bookie who would collect bets on sports that the inmates saw on the television. Whoever won the pool ended up tipping the bookie. There were the barbers who would cut your hair for a couple of racks of cookies. Packs of cookies, portable headphone radios, underwear, stamped envelopes, socks, they were all used as currency and if you could get your hands on some cigarettes, forget about it, you could name your price. Once in a while the inmates would sneak in some crack and smoke it with counterfeit pipes and lighters but Juan thought that was crazy; who in the hell would want to be all jittery and paranoid and with no alcohol or freedom? Juan did smoke some weed on one occasion and he enjoyed it thoroughly. His bunk was on the second floor and the correctional officers or CO's could not see it without coming up the stairs, so that made Juan's bunk prime real estate in the pod where he stayed. He rented it for a couple of racks or, in that occasion, for a high. He could also rent out his sneakers for a rack of cookies. If you didn't have sneakers you could not play basketball in the yard. Juan was a natural hustler so it was not a big adjustment to survive. If he survived the streets of his island, he could survive anywhere! He would play ping pong and was pretty good, which made him a favorite of some of the officers. Sometimes he would get one of the officers to sneak in some espresso coffee for him. Juan's wife would leave it on the bumper of the officer's car when she came to visit and the officer would bring it in and give it to the shop teacher, who would save it until Friday and then brew in the shop. They would drink coffee until they shit their pants, those boys in there would. It was a little taste of home for all of them. While in jail Juan decided to do something with his time and signed up for an experimental program that taught inmates auto repair. Eventually Juan passed all the certifications and became a teacher to other inmates. It was not easy, he had to carry a sharpened screw driver with him in the shop because once in a while an inmate would get violent and try to hurt him. He almost had to use it one time but the teacher took the guy away from Juan before he stabbed him. They both got lucky that time. Juan did not know how important this training would be in the future, it would put food on his table for a long time. The lessons about survival and heartbreak that Juan learned in there would save him many times in the future and would teach him about the evil that people were capable of, specially if they had power. He did not understand how so many people could be in jail for stupid stuff like a little marihuana, or driving without a license. It is expensive to keep someone locked up for stupid stuff like that. Of course, everybody was innocent, but there were a lot of people locked up for hearsay, specially when it came to domestic violence. If the cops showed up they said they had to arrest somebody, regardless of evidence and even if the neighbors made the call. They figured that the more people were put on probation to pay supervision, the safer their jobs were. Juan realized the pile of scumbags that these people were. Not all cops were bad in Juan's eyes, but there were enough of these publicly funded hoodlums with a badge that Juan wondered why they weren't fired. The answer was simple, they kept the economy moving, period. Lawyers made money, the courts made money, and the public supported it because they had a sense of security, after all, these were cops and they only arrested bad people, right?

There were times when Juan wondered if he was ever going to get out alive. At the beginning, when he still did not know the unspoken rules of doing time, he did not know how to approach people about conflicts in his cell. Like the time when there was an inmate who stank and apparently didn't know it. The right thing to do would have been for Juan to stand at the door of the cell and respectfully ask for his fellow inmates' attention and say that it appeared that the room was musty or that it smelled bad in there and that he was going to take a shower in case it was him. Juan was a little scared of saying anything because people get offended when you tell them they stink and it just so happened that the person who smelled bad was a 350 pound man. Juan was about 225 and strong but he didn't want to chance it, so he waited until the dope dealer on the top bunk said something about the smell. When the dope dealer came in the cell from taking a shower he said that it was musty in there. The smelly inmate asked the small white guy that was playing cards with him if he stank. It was almost comical to see the little white guy answer yes, he was shitting in his pants. So the big stinky guy gets up to go take a shower and after he exits the cell Juan says; "thank God!". Apparently the guy heard him and rushed back into the cell and started to come towards Juan telling him that if he needed to say something to say it to his motherfucking face. Juan was writing a letter to his wife and had a sharpened pencil in his hands and told the guy; "I'm sorry sir" with a cold heartless look in his eyes and the sharpened pencil in his right hand ready to stab the guy in the eye. The big guy backed up like he had seen the devil himself. Juan will always wonder what was it that the guy saw that made him turn pale and back up. After the guy took a shower he came into the room and told Juan he didn't want any trouble. Juan wonders what would have happened if the guy had not apologized; would he have stabbed him or beat him to a pulp in his sleep? He didn't know if it was over, he didn't know. An apology goes a long way in jail if it's done correctly. You can't be apologizing all the time though, it could be interpreted as weakness and then people will abuse you. Juan learned quickly though and he even became respected by other inmates. He stood his ground when someone tried to shake him for commissary or favors. It was not easy saying no to these individuals, some of them would not hesitate to try to take your property by force. One time he had to say no to an inmate who asked him for some food. The guy was close to seven feet tall and about 14 feet wide; he was huge! Later on that night, while Juan was on his knees praying, the big inmate started to walk towards Juan. The ground shook when this guy walked, he was that massive. Juan thought to himself that this was it, he was going to die tonight at the hands of this monster, but when the guy got close to Juan he asked him to pray for his mother. She was in her last days battling cancer and she probably was not going to make it through the night. His lawyer was trying to get him escorted to the hospital but was not successful. It was heartbreaking to see this man in pain and Juan promised him to pray for her. He never told anybody he had to change his underwear after praying though! It was good that Juan was tough, and that he had made good alliances not only with his Puertorican brothers, but the black and white people as well. Everybody learned that Juan would fight to the death, if necessary, for what he believed was right. Even when Juan broke his ankle playing ghetto ball in the yard, he stood up to people that tried him thinking he would not be able to defend himself. They tried him trying to disobey the unspoken agreement about voting for TV programs and Juan would just get up and disconnect it from the plug and face the rebellious inmates with his crutches and the support of his good friend José. José was a Puertorican gangster with a heart of gold and stainless steel balls. He had been a dope dealer in the area but this time he was set up for a burglary he did not commit. Juan and José went to church services in jail together and they could both sing pretty good. While talking about José's case, a south American inmate overheard the conversation and told them that he knew the guy who they were talking about and that he had worked for him. The went on to find out that this guy was being charged with a bunch of car thefts because of the same guy that had set José up. The south American guy told the guys where the guy's mother worked and Juan worked his magic on the guards to secure a phone call to the lady. They called her at her job from the jail and asked her to please contact her son so that José would not end up doing all that time for something her son did. She refused and played stupid. At the end of the day José refused to take the plea bargain for three years in prison and gambled it. He got ten years in prison for something he did not do. José and Juan remained friends for a long time and when Juan got out he would always send José a couple of dollars for commissary. Eventually they lost touch because José got lost in the system and Juan moved on with his life. I'm sure Juan would love to see his loyal friend again someday. They really became good friends. Another one of Juan's friends was a gay con artist named Omar. He was in jail for check fraud. This guy was making a thousand dollars a day with his check scam but got stupid and bought his boyfriend a Rolex from the wrong store. According to Omar you could not buy from certain stores. He told Juan the whole scam and Juan wrote on paper but lost it after a while. Juan did not intend to run the scam but there was something very interesting in learning crime from the actual criminal, no bullshit, just the truth. Being in jail taught Juan to not underestimate, to respect, to embrace fear as an ally, control it, concentrate it in a beam and push forward for survival. The images of violence, most of it igniting from a spark of fear, always stayed in Juan's head. He remembered the facial expression of the small, skinny black guy coming in the jail pod and five minutes later being handcuffed and carried out after beating the shit out of a huge black guy. The big guy had tried to intimidate the little guy, so the little guy put the combination lock to his locker inside one of his socks and hit the other guy with it. Juan always kept a couple of soap bars ready to put into his sock to swing at anybody who wanted to fuck with him. Anything went when it came to defending yourself in jail. Biting, eye gouging, stabbing, head butts, elbows, kicking, a chair, a pencil, grabbing, anything! Even though Juan would have liked to have never gone through this life changing experience, and to never think about it, the lessons learned in this torture chamber of sorts would save his life later on. Like the time when three robbers tried to do a home invasion on his house. He read them from the moment they called him on the phone to get him to come downstairs to look at their car at 9 pm. He analyzed their speech pattern, their accent, the speed of their words, their vocabulary, the content, correlated it with his street and jail wisdom, and in less than one second he had them waiting for him downstairs while he called 911 and got dressed at the same time. By the time they were trying to force their way into his house, he was already escaping out the back door. It was automatic, he detected danger automatically, it's like he smelled it. Thanks to that year and a half in jail he had gained a sixth sense and gained a trade. The lessons learned in jail were also about being considerate and respecting people's freedoms. People think inmates are all animals and have no morals or respect, when in fact it is the opposite. Most of these people are very sensitive humans who rebel against the insensitivity of the world towards the disenfranchised. In there Juan understood that it was a crime to wake an inmate from his sleep because it only time when he was free, that it was disrespectful to look out the window and later jerk off to someone else's wife. He learned from Puertorican inmates that was strictly prohibited in Puertorican prisons, as was going in the showers when the "women" were showering. The gay men in prison put brooms in the entrance of the showers to signal the fact that there were "women" in the premises and that you would have to wait or suffer a beating. Juan also heard how important it was in Puertorican prisons to guard the cell phones in there. It was the only way inmates had to communicate with their mothers because none of them could afford the gouging prices of collect calls from jail to them. Juan respected the inmates' audacity and wished he could go back and apologize to them for disrespecting them in the middle of an argument or by going back to jail after he was released and smoking a cigarette in the parking lot while the inmates watched. He knew how much they wanted a cigarette, that was not nice. Juan carried that guilt forever. Those people in there, most of them, were good people who had made stupid mistakes while enthralled in a fight with a weakness.

Juan left the jail during the Christmas season. He had gotten offered a plea bargain for a misdemeanor instead of a felony. His lawyer, the fourth one on his case, had exposed Jezebel for the person that she really was and had discovered that she had broken her aunt's leg on a rage, had stabbed a boyfriend over some money, had falsely accused one her 4 exes ,with whom she had children, of trying to hurt her so she could gain leverage in a custody battle with him. This woman was a real piece of work and Juan was the only one who stood up to her. He paid a steep price but Juan was used to fighting from his back ever since he was a little boy and lost his mother.

But the fight did not end when Juan walked out of the jail, it was just getting started. The Florida Department of Law Enforcement never updated his records and everywhere Juan went to find work it showed he was a convicted felon, even though he was not. Juan did not know this though. He just kept knocking on doors to try to get work. He first started in construction and later found work in a junkyard making 35 dollars a day pulling engines and transmissions. Later he found a better one making 50 dollars a day. He still had a lot to learn as far as being an auto mechanic, but he had the desire and the work ethic to make it. Later he found work in a national tire chain store, but noticed that if the business was slow he starved along with the business.

He did not like that so he left. He could not survive on 200 dollars a week while having to be at work for fifty hours. He thought it was that particular company that did that, but when he got a job at a Firestone store he found out the true meaning of a slave driving company. They paid him $9.50 an hour flat rate while they charged the customer almost a hundred. He had to buy his own tools and do all the work, and there were no scheduled times to go home, a gazillion hours at work and he only got paid when work came in. He had to go, Juan was not born to be a slave, so he started doing what he knew best; hustling. Only this time it was legal. He was going to get paid something decent for his hard work, no more giving corporate America his blood for peanuts. The state of Florida had stolen almost two years from him, but he decided to make lemonade out of lemons and use the training he got in jail to put a plate of food on his table. The long hours playing chess and listening to career criminals tell their stories had taught Juan many lessons on when to get out, get in, or when to pass. It's funny how humans have the capacity to thrive in many environments. I don't think Juan was proud of having gone to jail or that he enjoyed being incarcerated, but it showed him what he was capable of and how much strength was in him.

JUAN GETS A PROSTATE TEST

When Juan was married with his first wife, him and his wife had been trying to get pregnant but never succeeded. Juan's wife decided that they had to go and see a fertility doctor. Juan shows up at the doctor's office in the morning and fills out the paperwork and stuff. A few minutes later a nurse hands Juan a little plastic vial and tells him to give her a sample of his semen. She asks him if he is going to require some help and he very happily says YES! Juan is thinking that this girl is going to take him into a room and give him a blowjob or and hand job. The nurse comes back with a couple of porn magazines and hands them to Juan. What a disappointment for Juan! What type of subpar patient care were these people running in this sperm shop? Thought Juan. So Juan goes in the little jerking off room and puts his flagellated friends in it and delivers them to the nurse. She instructs him to go into an examination room and wait for the doctor. The doctor walks in and greets him. He is a young Colombian. He tells Juan to pull his pants down so he can examine his testicles and penis. Everything is fine, says the doctor. Now he tells Juan to turn around and bend over. Here is where Juan has a problem. He tells the doctor that he is here for a fertility test and not a prostate test. The doctor says that the prostate test is part of it. Juan tells him that if he had known he would have brought a negligee and a flower bouquet with him. So Juan bends over ready to lose his virginity to this complete stranger who didn't even take him to dinner or paid him a compliment, such rudeness! The doctor puts his gloves on and takes a handful of lubricant gel and plasters Juan's behind with it. He then sticks his finger up Juan's butt and starts poking at his prostate. As soon as Juan felt that inside him he almost shit himself. He started yelling at the doctor; "hurry up or I'll shit on you!, hurry, hurry, oh my God!" . The doctor finished and Juan told him that he had no idea how close he had come to being shit on! Juan cleaned the excess lubricant off his butt and proceeded to walk out of that cubicle with his butt cheeks doing a weird dance due to the lubricant. Yuck!, thought Juan. Everything was fine, said the doctor, he was very fertile and he could have kids. Now Juan knew that he was straight, he could never have a boyfriend, there is no way he could do the reverse dance. And to think that people think that you could turn into gay, Juan knew better; gay people are born that way.

JUAN ENTERS THE CAR WORLD

Juan's first job after getting out of jail was in a junkyard getting parts off of cars for 35 bucks a day in the late 90's. It was brutal and dangerous work. He worked for this Iranian crack head who would rip off his own mother. It was the first thing that came up and he had no money. He slowly built up a little clientele on the side and worked on their cars after work. He later got a raise and went to work for another junkyard making 50 dollars a day. From there he met another Iranian who owned a car dealer and became his mechanic/salesperson. Juan was always hustling a sale and he was really good with people. The only thing that killed his profits was the fact that he negotiated for the buyer against his boss. The place was pretty much a junkyard with a few cars that were in shape for sale. The rest of the cars had blown engines, or trannies, or needed major repairs. Juan started buying cars with blown engines from the Iranian. He fixed them and sold them for a profit. Little by little he started saving up and bought himself a couple of cars at a time and sold them. He had to jump titles (sell the cars without registering them under his name) because Florida only allowed people to sell three cars under their name per year. It was a way to protect the gazillion dealers who scammed the public in Florida. Dealers had lobbied the lawmakers for exclusivity and, as usual, had gotten what they paid for; tax payer funded legislators who worked for them by pimping the tax payer to their interests. If the people violated the law they were subject to stiff penalties and even jail! God bless America!

Eventually Juan decided to try his hand at selling cars so he applied at a Mazda dealership not knowing if they were going to hire him because of his domestic violence conviction. They did! Juan had never sold cars at a dealership and he still had the buyer's advocate mentality. He sold 15 cars his first month but did not make much money because he would negotiate the prices in favor of the customers. This took money out of his pocket. He did not last long selling cars for a dealer. He refused to lie to people like the managers told him to do. He hated to see people abused. Some times the salespeople would take the keys to the car the customer wanted to trade in and hide them if the negotiations stalled. This would give the manager time to sweeten the deal and get the sale. Juan would never work for a dealership again as a salesperson. He did as a mechanic but they started trying to give him work that was supposed to be done by the higher level technicians because he was getting paid less and could do the high level repairs. Car dealers always had a way to screw people, even their employees. Juan tried his hand at a couple of other places; Firestone, Tires Plus, a couple of independent shops, but it was always the same. All of them wanted Juan to sell the customer items that did not need replacing. They all wanted to screw him over too. They paid him the lowest flat rate hour possible even though he deserved more. They would charge the customer 80 dollars per labor hour and pay Juan $9.50 per labor hour, even though he did all the work with his own tools. If the shops did not have enough work they would just pay Juan the minimum of $5.15 per hour. Juan had had enough and did what he knew how to do best; go hustle a dollar, only this time he used his skills in a legal way. He got a license to do auto repairs and started knocking on doors to offer his services as a mobile auto technician. He first had a little four cylinder Plymouth duster. He bought it for a hundred bucks and fixed up a couple of things. He would get pulled over all the time for a busted tail light and for being of the wrong race and in the wrong neighborhood (most of his customers were from suburbia). The cops eventually stopped bothering him once they knew him. They knew he was the mechanic and Juan always told them that they wanted 175 dollars for the taillight at the store(which was true) and that that was more than he paid for the car! They would always laugh and let him go. He then bought an old BMW two door with a fuel injection problem that he rigged because the car would not stay running at stop lights. He had to flip a switch he installed to keep the fuel pressure switch closed until it was time to go. Juan eventually got a loan from his uncle and bought some equipment and a little van where he had all his tools. Him and his wife bought a house, and things were running along smooth. He later started to build rotary engine race cars after his friend Shorty taught him how to work on them. He became quite famous for his junkyard Frankenstein creations. He had the ugliest and dirtiest little import racers that would beat the nicely painted 69 Camaros at the track. He would race his

Frankenstein cars for a couple of years until the fever left him. After that he kept working on cars and once in a while would buy a fixer upper to resell. Juan knew that he didn't want to keep working on cars the rest of his life; it was hard work and his back would hurt all the time. He knew that he could make more money with his brain. The trick was to get a job in a good company that would let him use his creativity and amazingly powerful brain. It was easier said than done. He had a bachelors degree but employers in Florida didn't give a rats ass about it. Everybody wanted to pay you 10 dollars an hour without benefits. All the jobs they offered him were as a phone jockey or as a professional legal thief (time share resale, time share sale, car sales, utility sales, insurance sales, credit card processing sales, vacation sales, etc). Many of the job offers were 100% commission and 1099, which meant that Juan had to pay for all the gas, wear and tear on his car, insurance, license plate, license fees, food while on the road, and advertising and effort out of his pocket until he made a sale. Then, on top of that, he had to pay 35 percent of his income, after paying 15.3% FICA tax on the gross income. It did not make any sense to him, it was costing him money to work! Juan said; fuck these people!

Juan later went and got a real estate license to sell a house to his cousin and tried his hand at real estate for about six months. True to form, Juan got into a business just when it was bad. It was almost at the end of the housing bubble and you could not find any houses to buy. People were having to offer 10 to 15 grand on top of the asking price if they wanted to have a chance of winning the bidding wars that ensued. Juan finally found a house for his cousin and she paid him under the table. Eventually Juan went back to hustling auto repair and referring people to his friends who had dealers. They would give him a few hundred dollars for the lead and he was happy because he didn't have to invest to make the money. Juan grew tired of the fixing cars and wanted out but could not leave it. Florida was brutal when it came to managerial or good jobs for ex cons. Juan always dreamed of getting a good job or hitting it big with one of his ideas and finding an angel to sponsor him. He loved cars but he knew that his body was going to quit on him someday soon and would have to stop working on cars. He was not making much money anyway, he barely survived. He did not understand how the hell the government wanted income tax from him, he barely made his bills. Whenever he got a good repair he took his son Daniel to the Chucke Cheese and to the putt putt place and buy him a toy or a book. He figured that the accountant would cost him 1,200 a year just to tell him that he did not owe any money. He chose to spend that money on his little boy, he needed shoes and clothing and food. He wasn't paying into his social security account and that worried him, but he figured that before long something would turn around and he would be able to pay into it. He had done some credit card processing sales for a little and was getting about 50 dollars a month in residuals. He stopped that gig because the company he was selling for started charging the people he signed up for the service 150 dollars a year without the people's consent. Juan would sign them on for the service and a month later the company would send them a letter saying that unless they sent the company a letter refusing the extra 150 dollars a year charge, they would be signed on into it. The company also failed to tell the clients that the contracts would renew themselves automatically unless the client cancelled it. This pissed Juan off and he stopped selling for the company. He just wished they told the people up front. He brought this problem to the attention of the manager but he told Juan that everybody was doing it, so it was OK. Juan coined a phrase for these companies; Scammerican companies. And he despised all their nefarious tactics. Funny thing, Juan had been a dope fiend and a male prostitute to support his habit, he drove around in a couple of cars that Loco had stolen, sold dope, stole a couple of small things, and even dealt in a few stolen things, but he didn't burn people. The one or two times he took something from someone it was because one of his Johns would not pay him or something like that. He did steal a couple of toys when he was a young boy because his friends did it, so he wanted to fit in. He did not like it though, Juan was not a thief, he would rather beg. Juan did not hate the people in the game, he hated the game and understood that some of these salespeople had no choice but to keep living in their grey area; they had too many bills. Juan always liked to give something for something or vice-versa. He found out that there is peace in being a stand up guy. He really loved it. The one thing that being a mechanic gave Juan was the ability to fix people's problems, be needed, and get paid for honest work. The joy he got from fixing a car that no one else could fix was magnanimous. People paid him happily. It was not easy though, he had to weed out the cheap people and the thieves. He stopped doing work for dealers because they always wanted Juan to "doctor" the cars just enough to sell them. One time he saw a couple of dealers sell a single mother a car for her daughter. It was her first car and they had put in a head gasket treatment to make it run for a little. That broke Juan's heart. He remembered the sacrifices his mother had to make to take care of him and he wanted no part in conning a person, not even a bad person. He also stopped advertising in Spanish radio because most of the customers he got were really poor, and as much as he wanted to help them, he still had to feed himself and his loved ones. Juan was Puertorican and he loved his people, he just wished so many of them were not so broke and cheap. He laughed when he told me; "look Ray, if you want to do business with us Puertoricans, you need to either sell us Mercedes Benz cars at full price, or 99 cent shit that we don't need and is trending, everything else we are going to try to get for free or at a deep discount with a lifetime money back guarantee". Juan did not know it at the time, but his life and the lives of all his loved ones, were about to change. His ferociousness about love, and the disenfranchised would take him to a place of power and freedom, which is the essence of power, which would give him peace. Not because of the power, but because for one time it would be put to good use. But not yet, not yet. He had to be polished by pain, frustration, darkness, loneliness, and depression, one more time. He found out that life is like a 1974 Mazda RX-4. It was beautiful, you had to change gears, make it more powerful through modifications, it looked different from every angle and light situation, needed maintenance, and if you were smart, you would find someone to drive and maintain it for you just for the pleasure of driving it and showing it. You would also split the profits it made from the shows and pay for the maintenance from them. That was Juan and his wisdom.

JUAN'S FRIEND TIPPER

Tipper was a commercial jumbo jet pilot gone bad. He liked his cocaine and booze more than anything and it drove him to lose his commercial pilot's license. He had always been a fat guy but boy did he pull some panties down or what? This guy had bunnies spread out all over the place, US, the Caribbean, you name it. He had the gastric bypass surgery and it almost killed him because a mistake from one of the doctors made his intestines infarct. They saved him after he was in a coma for a month. Tipper and Juan met at a 12 step meeting and Juan had never seen anybody more inappropriate or resourceful than Tipper. It was funny to see Tipper hire his hookers and then try to get them clean by bringing them to meetings. Hey, he was showing a good heart. Juan guessed he was trying to save the girls from their pimps and the street, and that was cool by Juan. Tipper once went for a job interview as a manager in a small airline but got rejected by a very nasty female manager because of his rap sheet, so he went and sold all his properties and bought the company. He then went to the office and looked at the nasty manager and told her she was fired for being a bitch to him during the interview. Juan loved it because he had suffered the same rejection from employers because he had a conviction for domestic violence.

Tipper could not stay clean for more than a year or so at a time. He always ended up getting high with his hooker girlfriends. I mean, Juan did not judge him, this guy was not good looking, so the only company he could find was the one he could pay for, which is really no different than many other guys out there, they just don't know it. He just was not interested in the games that the non declared hookers played. His favorite one was one really hot chic with a boyfriend. Her boyfriend worked for Tipper stealing merchandise from major home improvement retailers and then returning it in exchange for gift cards. Tipper would then buy the gift cards from the boyfriend at a 50% discount and sell them online for 85% of the face value. Tipper had about five or six dope fiends all over the tri-county area doing the same. He was making about 5,000 dollars a week profit and had no bills because his house was paid off. Tipper had a talent for making money quick.

Juan's relationship with Tipper was a bit adversarial because he saw so many of his own flaws in Tipper that it pissed him off. Juan also was a little envious of Tipper's ability to make money so easy, but he knew that it was dirty money and that eased his pain. Juan did not know it but he really appreciated his friend and had developed a profound caring love for this brave soul. He really wished he had the capital to invest and make Tipper his general manager and get him out of the street hustle and into a legitimate corporate place where he could shine. But that was not to be. Tipper would die under suspicious circumstances in his early fifties. It was very painful for Juan to have his dear friend die. Some say he took an overdose of painkillers, others say his hooker girlfriend gave him too much yeyo, who knows? The cops did not want to investigate, they did not care about a street hustling ex-junkie waking up dead next to his crack head hooker girlfriend. I bet you if a dog from a prominent family had died under suspicious circumstances they would have investigated.

DARBY THE GREEK

Darby was American by birth, and Puertorican by injection. She had Greek and Irish blood with an ass that would not quit. She grew up in New York near the Hasidic Jewish neighborhoods. Her and her friends would rob the Jewish older men of their money. She knew that they hid their money in their hats, and the bigger the hat the more money they had. She and her friend would get friendly with the target and lure them into an alley with the promise of a blowjob from a young white girl with deep blue eyes, black hair, perky titties and a tight sweet butt. When they got their target into the alley they pulled out a knife and took his hat off to take the money in it and ran. It was like a sport to them. They would even sell baby cocaine(baby powder in a baggie) to a blind guy telling him it was the real deal. Darby went to school to be a registered nurse and was very good at it. She married a young American business executive of Arab descent. This was the most decent guy you could ever meet, he would give you the shirt off his back. They had three boys and lived comfortably in suburbia. Darby never could shake her bad girl habits though. Throughout the years she would have flings here and there and go on coke binges. Eventually, all the cocaine binging progressed to a place where it was causing severe problems with Darby's work and family. She ended up going to NA meetings and started to get clean and sober. While there Juan introduced her to one of his Puertorican friends called Johnny. That was all she wrote; these two hooked up in a ferocious tornado of an affair that had them living together in about two weeks. Darby left her husband and filed for divorce so fast that everybody's jaws touched the floor. She was in your face about it too. She would take her boys to school everyday and went about business as usual like nothing happened. Her kids were thrown for a loop but eventually would understand that their mother was just like that; honest, with no bullshit in her, brave, and a fighter. In hindsight she did the best thing for her and her husband, let him be free. After about a year of being with Johnny, he went back to using drugs and drinking. She was devastated and came to Juan crying. She told Juan she could not believe that Johnny had done this to her. Juan, being the honest prick that he was, told her "you did the same thing to your husband for many years, it sucks when they do it to you don't it?". She could not believe Juan was telling her the truth in such a horribly blunt way. Darby cursed Juan out and ran away from him crying. She came back to him the next day and Juan explained to her that he had to be brutal in order to get her to see the reality. Throughout the next 7 or 8 years Darby and Johnny continued to see each other and have more drama. Johnny would beat up Darby or go on a binge and Darby would come back to Juan with the same story; "I will never go back to him, blah blah" and Juan would tell her that he would give her a week before they were back together. And he would be right every time. Juan knew this because he was just like Darby when it came to people he loved, he forgave them to a fault. He had gone through the same thing with Lucía. Johnny would go to jail all the time on dope and domestic violence charges and Darby would always dump whoever she was with to be with him. She would try to date other men to get Johnny out of her system but it never worked. Her and Juan even tried to date to see if they were compatible but could never have sex because Juan and her would start laughing the one time they took their clothes off in front of each other. They were friends! Johnny had introduced her to crack and it damn nearly killed her. She ended up getting in trouble with the law for stealing. What saved her was her persistence with trying to get clean. She finally achieved it with AA, the help of a psychiatrist, and the fact that Johnny got a 6 year prison sentence. Juan would always check up on her and was worried that she would get back together with Johnny after he got out of prison. For the time being though, she seemed to be happy with her new boyfriend. She had conquered a lot of demons and was now starting a new business and a new life. She had been clean for a few years and life was looking good. Her boys were being teenage boys and her ex had found love in another woman and they all got along fairly well. Juan always thought he would put Darby up in a section of his farm for rejects of society, just like him. Or maybe even make her head of operations of his hotel business in the US. She had the talent to find rich people and make them happy. Juan learned a lot of lessons in loyalty and perseverance from Darby, those two will always be friends, no matter what! In the days when Juan could not afford to see a doctor she would use her contacts in the medical field to get Juan his anti-depressants, or Nexium, or antibiotics. She was always looking out for Juan's health and his feelings. They still go to jazz festivals together and Darby makes sure her boyfriends meet Juan's big ass, just in case they are getting any ideas of getting stupid with her; Juan doesn't play when it comes to Darby's safety and security, it's kind of comical how he protects her, but then again, that's just who Juan is, a big protector. What did end up happening was that Darby opened up a high end assisted living facility for women who had drug problems. Her clientele was 50% rich people but she kept the other half of the available beds open to street, disadvantaged women. It was her way of staying true to her heart and compassion for those in need, Darby had a big heart. Juan financed the facility and shared in the profits, which were decent and provided Darby with a good life for her boys. Darby also had a division of her business that focused on educating her clients on arts and crafts that they could sell on their website and stores and use the money to better themselves and send money to their children. If they did not have contact with their kids because they had given them away or lost them to the courts, they would donate some of the money to the charities who ran orphan programs and also to the child support offices in their respective states. It was funny, they would just walk in with a big wad of cash into the courthouses and just hand them over to the clerks. They later started to send them checks but at the beginning they just took cash. Everybody called them cash mommas. The one project that was the real pet for both Juan and Darby was a runaway teenager protection network called "Runaway Angels". Juan and Darby both knew the dangers runaway teenagers were exposed to, especially the girls. From pimps, dirty cops, judgmental religious freaks, serial killers, gangs, sex enslavers, foreign underground rings, you name it, these girls were targets. Darby knew a lot of street people who had gotten clean and were now unemployed and had to resort to work underground to make a living because they had criminal records for prostitution, drug possession, and stuff like that. These women all had lost custody of their children through their lifestyle but were all loving people. It's just that their addiction exerted a heavy toll on them. Darby spread the word out on the street that if you were a runaway you could go to certain safe houses and get a plate of food, take a shower, get some clean clothes, and sleep for up to twelve hours and hit the road again. There were no questions asked, no pressure, no judgment. The houses had private security visit them randomly and if the runaways wanted to turn themselves in they could do so, if not, they could leave freely. Darby and Juan understood that some of these kids were running from abusive parents, or adoptive, or foster parents. Some were being passed around the foster parents' friends like a joint, or used as slave labor wherever the system put them. To turn them in forcefully would be to sentence them to more of the same. Runaway angels became sort of an underground railroad for kids who had lost faith in humanity. It was financed by donations from former runaways who had made it out alive and by the Bill and Melinda Gates foundation. Darby and Juan were both nominated for a medal in civil service, Darby won it and went to the white house to accept it. In the middle of a sea of tears and sobs she urged parents to not give up on their children even if they had given up on themselves. It was a good day in Washington DC, the sun was out, it was in the fifties, and Darby, Juan, María, and a bunch of rejects from society had shown the world that love can turn anyone into a hero...

JUAN TRIES TO BECOME A NURSE

Juan did not have health insurance when he got his vertigo attacks, so he did what everybody does when they get sick these days; hit the internet for information. He was fascinated with medicine right away. He was good with machines and the human body is a machine. He would stay online for a gazillion hours investigating the vestibular apparatus. He would just start digesting information at a frantic pace. It was like a drug to him. He had an epiphany, what if he went to school and went into the medical field? He went to the University of Central Florida and applied for readmission and got it. He got his loans re-instated and started taking two classes at a time. He started with chemistry, which he hadn't taken in twenty years, and also signed up for pre-med biology. His first day of class was nerve wrecking, he felt so out of place with all these kids around. He did not think he had what it took anymore. His clinical depression made it very hard for him to focus and read all this material and understand it. He remembered when he used to be able to learn while drunk. It was not like that anymore. His brain was not as fast as it used to be and his mental health was not very good but he kept pushing. The chemistry was brutal, the professor was a crazy Panamanian guy who could barely speak English and really sucked at teaching. He was a very nice guy with serious control issues and Juan learned to appreciate his bravery. Juan refused to go to tutoring sessions, he wanted to prove to himself that he could do it all on his own. He ended up getting a "B" plus in the class only to find out that he did not need to take that high of a level chemistry to go into nursing. You see, Juan was thinking about taking all the necessary courses to try for a medical school but realized that his chances of getting into one in the US were pretty much zero. He did not have a good GPA because he had dedicated himself to drugs and alcohol during his early college years, had a misdemeanor criminal conviction, didn't have the money, and was on his own, without anyone backing him. After weighing his options, he decided to go for nursing. He could have gone to Spain, or the Caribbean, but that would have required being away from Daniel for long periods of time and he was not going to do that. No matter what, he was going to stay close to his son, to his king. Juan took an anatomy class that almost drove him nuts and became good friends with the doctor who taught it. He later took physiology, microbiology, all the laboratories, sociology, human development, etc. When he was two classes short of completing the pre-requisites for applying to a nursing school the government changed the rules for financial aid. Juan had one bachelor's degree already and he was going for a second one. The republican controlled congress decided that people did not need second bachelor's degrees or to retrain, and took their loans away. Juan was pissed but there was nothing he could do. After all his efforts and an additional 20 grand in student loans, he was back to having to bust his ass under the sun working on cars to make a living (not that he ever stopped). Juan could go to law school or get a master's degree, but Juan was exhausted from school, from so many closed doors, so many heartbreaks, so many fucking lemons. He felt like he just wanted to quit, to grab a stupid job that paid him crap, where his talent would languish, and his soul would perish, and just watch movies about people who went for their dreams. He almost felt like just getting fucked up and enjoying the high, but he tried that once and it did not work. He knew the the story of self pity ended in self destruction. He really wished he could just let go of all his sorrow and frustration and be happy with what he had, and cultivate his talents, regardless of the outcome. To sow just for the joy of sowing, regardless of the crop. It was like he was cursed, he thought. But he did not understand that he just had to let go of his expectations and follow his passions and the rest would follow. I guess he thought that all that crap people said about letting go and letting God was useless and it led to complacency. I don't blame him. Juan was not born to be complacent, he had to innovate and develop or he felt like he was dead inside. If he could just find out who to sell all his lemons to...

JUAN GETS TWO MILLION DOLLARS FOR HIS UNIVERSITY

Juan had decided to go and get a nursing degree because he had found a passion for the medical field. He already knew he wanted to help humans who were sick, he had a heart of gold. His passion was also helped along by an unexpected turn for the worst in his health. At 37 years old Juan started to feel the effects of the abuse he had put his body through when he was younger. He had developed a bad ulcer, gained about 40 pounds, and his anxiety and depression were kicking his ass.

He had been taking anti-depressants for a while now and still felt anxious and depressed sporadically. He had gone to the poor man's doctor, the internet, and found out he had all the symptoms of ADD, ADHD, and PTSD. He did not have health insurance since losing his last job and the prospect of finding a good paying job with insurance was really low. He developed periodontal disease, obesity, peptic ulcers, GERD, chronic esophaghitis and gastritis, chronic obstructive pulmonary disease, heel spurs on his left ankle, benign positional vertigo, ulcerative colitis, hemorrhoids, insomnia, sleep apnea, and just generally felt like shit most of the time. He paid for the university insurance but they determined through their crystal ball method that everything was pre-existing and did not cover any of the tests after they said they would. It was like Juan was being punished for rolling all those joints with miniature new testament paper. At least that's what he always tells me. So Juan got all these diagnostics and also got stuck with the medical bills. Juan still rages on about the rip-off medical system that exists in this country. You pay for a service that is never intended to be given and the government and the morons from political parties support the denial. Juan tells me it's like genocide based on socio-economic status, only the ones who can afford expensive medical care get to survive.

Juan woke up one thanksgiving morning and when he sat up on his bed the whole room started to spin and he went into uncontrollable puking that took his strength from him. He could not move his head without puking non-stop. His ears started to ring loudly and he felt very sick. His roommate urged him to go to the hospital but Juan did not want to go, he didn't have insurance. Juan finally called his girlfriend at the time and she took him to the ER. He slowly made his way into the triage area with a bucket in his hands to puke into. When the doctor saw him she made him lay on the stretcher and raised his feet up a little. She then turned his head to the left but nothing happened. When she turned his head to the right, he started puking like the girl from the exorcist, and would not stop dry heaving, it was awful. She diagnosed him with benign positional vertigo and put him on parenteral Benadryl along with an anti-emetic. Juan discovered some exercises on the internet to help him with the vertigo but he stayed dizzy for about a month and his ears would not stop ringing. After that attack he recovered and thought he was OK. He continued to smoke cigarettes and live normally, but about six months later, while working under a car, he felt like the car was going to run him over even though it was mounted on jack stands. He knew he had another attack and this time he would stay dizzy for about three months. He remembers having to go underneath a car praying that he did not get another vertigo attack, or going to Miami with Felo to buy a hearse for his uncle's funeral parlor and driving it all the way to north Florida for shipping. He was so dizzy that he had to keep one eye closed to stay on the road. He figured if he crashed and died he was already inside the hearse. Several months later he took an over the counter sexual stimulant and had a severe allergic reaction and felt like he was going to die. The reaction came back a couple of times and it kept him in the hospital for a week. He basically felt like he was out of breath after he took a couple of steps and felt dizzy. Juan was tired of feeling sick and getting new symptoms all the time. He had medical insurance for a few months and did all the tests he could; cat scans, mri to rule out ms, heart studies, blood work. The only thing the doctors found were small nodules in Juan's lungs that would disappear after a session of antibiotics. Later on Juan started developing small post-inflammatory scars at the bottom of his right lung but the doctors just told him to lose weight. Eventually Juan gave up on the doctors and went to the license bureau and took off his organ donor status. He wanted to get an autopsy when he died so that his family and science could find out what was wrong with him and know that he was not faking it. Juan also registered for a second bachelor's degree and found the school where he went to an awesome place for research and learning. He learned about some new treatments being developed to cure children's diseases and decided to write the Bill Gates foundation and ask for money for his school. Juan also started writing scientists at the school about ideas he had to conquer AIDS. Juan learned that HIV came from monkeys and that monkeys did not get sick from it, so he wrote the main immunologist at the university and gave him the idea to search for the answer in monkeys' blood. After all, the virus had come from monkeys and their immune system had figured out a way to live with virus in harmony. The faculty started doing research on it immediately and around the same time the Bill Gates foundation gave his school two million dollars for research. They did not even send Juan a thank you email from the University after getting the money but Juan knew that his actions had saved a lot of children's lives and that made him be at peace. Juan was used to being the underdog, the unsung hero, the lemonade master.

JUAN'S FRIEND JADEN

In one of his visits to his shrink Juan met this lady who worked there. She was in her early sixties and was very nice towards him. They always conversed when he went there. One day he received a letter without return address with a lottery ticket in it. He did not know who had sent it but had a hunch it had been Jaden. The next time he went to the office they exchanged phone numbers and started calling each other and talking on the phone. Jaden wanted Juan to do her and she came out and told him, not in those words, but in a very honest manner. Juan very politely declined but told her he wanted to be friends with her. She was persistent though, she told Juan that there was a good possibility he could get in her daughter's pants if he slept with her. That sounded interesting to Juan but he still did not bite. He met Jaden's daughter and he preferred to earn the chance by himself if he ever decided to go for it. Jaden had two daughters, one was a lesbian and the other an executive partner in a law firm. The executive one was very pretty and snobbish and the other was just plain not interesting to Juan. Jaden had been a high price escort in her younger days. She held a job with the federal government during the weekdays and would hook on the weekends. She managed to buy a few houses and put her kids through school with the extra money she earned. Her kids, however, judged and shunned her when they found out what her mother used to do for a living on the weekends. They never gave her the respect she deserved. Juan felt a lot of respect for Jaden and really wanted to help her with her life. One time, after Jaden had a heart attack, Juan went to visit her. She had quit working at the clinic and was looking for a job. Jaden had told Juan that she was sick of living and wanted to commit suicide and that she was going to do it at the beach. She even took him to the spot where she said she was going to slit her wrists open. Juan did not panic and tried to talk her out of it, but it was like talking to a wall. That night, after coming back from the beach, Juan called Jaden's daughter and left a message in her phone warning her of her mothers intentions. Back at Jaden's house Juan sat on Jaden's bed listening to her while she talked and drank some vodka. She had given a blow job to this Italian guy who kept hounding her about sex. She had charged him 200 dollars and bought some vodka with it. I guess Jaden was just tired of all the bullshit in her life; the ungratefulness of her children towards her, the not making the same amount of money she used to make, the having gotten old and see her body deteriorate. Juan pitied her but above all came to love her as a human being. She found herself a good man from a northern native American tribe and moved in with him and his dog. They spoke a couple of more times on the phone and then lost contact. He always respected her determination to raise her children. She even drove tractor trailers at one time to put food on her family's table, such courage! Maybe one day they would run into each other and have some coffee, but it's OK for Juan if they don't, Jaden taught him some courage and some true love, you couldn't ask for more.

JUAN BECOMES A FATHER

Juan's best friend had asked him to take care of her little three year old boy while she went to Reno with her dying mother and her brother to take her mother to a big casino vacation as a last wish. Juan accepted the request gladly. He had been there when the boy was born, even witnessed the doctor doing the cesarean section. He held the boy in his hands before his mother did. He cried, laughed, yelled, jumped, sighed, became breathless, all at once, when he saw the boy and held him in his hands. They named him Daniel, after his great grandfather. All throughout the pregnancy nobody knew who the real father was because even though Juan was supposed to be the donor, Juan's friend had started dating a man at the same time Juan had donated his seed to impregnate his friend Brenda. The agreement was that Juan was going to be the donor but still would be a father to the kid. It was kind of weird for Juan to not know who the daddy was going to be, but it didn't matter to Juan, he already loved the kid, which was going to be a miracle kid because he knew that the chances of Brenda getting pregnant were almost Zero.

Juan had been friends with Brenda for a long time and had even dated her for a while. It didn't work out, they were way too different, or maybe too much alike, who knows? They did, however, remained best of friends and could count on each other without questions. Some people, when they learned about this non-conventional pregnancy, started with their opinions but Juan set them straight really fast and eliminated them from his list of friends. Fuck 'em if they were going to judge, he thought. As far as Juan was concerned, all life came from love and that made love God to Juan. The rest of the religions were nothing more than a bunch of genocidal mythologies to Juan; all they did was to stick humans in classes and burn those who didn't agree, some at the stake, some in hell, some in the unemployment lines. Juan had matured into a fiercely combative human who fought with his pen and tongue against all those who mobbed against freedom of lifestyle, free love, and the oneness of humanity. He had developed a phobia for hypocrisy, demagogy, apathy, abuse, and blind fanaticism. He learned that his passions could get him to become what he despised, so he constantly checked the lessons learned through his mistakes, against established principles in his idiosyncrasy. Nothing could be absolute other than his resolution to improve himself through feeding the good dog inside of him, not the bad one. Juan had the capacity to love deeper than any human could, which also made him capable of hating and reaching for a scorn that could wipe out civilizations. This scared him, to be able to reach so deep. He sometimes thought he was unique in this ability, but through educating himself he learned that this was a very human trait, and that those that conquered this flaw could be of great light in the darkness of the history of humanity. He knew he had the opportunity to love deeper than he ever thought a human could, because when he saw the opportunity to hate he chose to unleash his passion for the love of this little boy. When the boy was born Juan saw that he looked just like his father, and it wasn't Juan. He wasn't disappointed or relieved like some people said he should be, for not having to pay child support that is. Instead, he was in a kind of stupor at witnessing this life that he saw in the sonograms and felt kick through Brenda's belly. He saw the helplessness of this little boy lying in a cold room with a blanket around his body and a wool cap on his little head. He knew that his job was to protect him and care for him if the boy ever needed him.

It turned out that the father was nowhere to be found when the mother gave birth. He also wasn't there when they had to operate the boy at two weeks old for a birth defect. Juan never forgot holding this little boy in his hands with tubes stuck in his nose and an IV line on his little foot. The boy's mother asked Juan to be there for help and support but when she would go downstairs for a cigarette, Juan could not stop sobbing at the sight of this baby in his hands with all these tubes and machines getting him ready for an operation.

Juan's friend ended up moving the boy's biological father in with her. She had fallen in love with him but he didn't really care. To him she was just a convenience thing. He was illegally in the country and she was a citizen with a large bank account and a comfy house. Juan had paid 600 dollars for the paternity test even though he knew the baby did not carry his blood. When he found out officially he called the father and congratulated him. He also asked him to let him see the boy from time to time and offered himself to help if ever needed. Juan was a class act inside, all love. It was just the outside that was rough. He had to be, life, being an ex-con and ex-junkie, had a tendency to spit on his face more often than not.

The boy's father turned out to have some problems that Juan had conquered in the past, namely cocaine and alcohol abuse. The father would go on binges and disappear for three days. Brenda would call Juan for advice on how to help this guy, but they both knew what had to be done. She had to kick this guy out and let him have his bottom. But that was easier said than done. There was always the risk of him getting deported and the boy losing his father. He could not come back into the country due to some dope charges that he had in the past. It was always scary for the family when he went out to work.

Juan had gotten a job as a sales executive in his uncle's company, but it didn't work out. After spending almost a year battling a very dishonest and conniving partner of his uncle, he decided it was better for him to go than to flush this guy down a toilet like he deserved. By the time he went back to the town where Brenda and the baby lived, the baby's father had been deported to his country. The little boy, Daniel, was about three by then and was aware that something was wrong. He was hurt because his father was gone. Juan made sure he spent as much time as he could with the boy and on one of those times the boy asked him if he was his daddy. Juan asked him if he wanted him to be his daddy and the boy answered yes. So Juan told him he would be his daddy and Daniel hugged himself and let out a very loving "daddy". It was so beautiful and at the same time so heart wrenching to see this boy do this that Juan just started crying. He would never forget that moment of pure love from a three year old. So profound, so easy, so true. Juan told Brenda about the promise he made to the boy and she was OK with it. She was still in love with the father but knew it was not to be. South America was a dangerous place those days and she was not going to follow the guy into the third world. She and Juan would not get back together even though they considered it. They were not compatible even though they cared about each other. Juan felt at home every time he went to see the boy, so much so that he stayed overnight when he did. Juan even dumped a few women who had a problem with him staying with his boy at Brenda's. He had no time for bullshit in his life, his little boy came first, period!

Juan always told me that if he had money he would pay off the boy's mother's house and buy a farm for them to live in. He would even open a business for the mother to run or something, so that she would not have to work so hard. Anything to help them. He did not know it but his words were prophetic. He would open a foundation that took care of children born in the USA and whose parents had been deported. Juan tried lobbying with politicians to make special exceptions for visitation between kids and their deported parents but it was not to be. The politicians did not want to risk losing the vote from their southern evangelical racist constituency. Juan eventually struck a deal with a few Californian border towns to build visitation hotels for these families and their deported loved ones. The federal government did not intervene, even though the tea party and the rest of the extreme right wing idiots rallied against it. Juan's little experiment turned into a huge cash moving machine, only this time it was truly a work of love that spawned an entire new industry; deportation tourism. The hotels were in the US side of the border and the governments of Mexico and US would profit from it legally. Security was very tight on both sides, including drug screenings for everyone and the whole process was monitored from start to finish. In order to enter the hotels you had to have a special access card and be identified with a biometric signature in a national database. Once inside the compounds where the hotels were, parents and children would be reunited in the big lobby. There were clowns and people available to take pictures of the kids with their parents. There was a huge playground with all sorts of kid's toys. The hotels had movie theaters, and little malls with items from both sides of the border. There were volunteer psychologists and physicians on staff at all times in case anyone got sick. Juan's foundation covered the cost for most families who could not afford the experience. Daniel's biological father became an employee of Juan's foundation in South America and would communicate with Daniel a lot through the Tango application on his smart phone. Daniel's love had accomplished what governments had failed to do because of fear of hatred and ignorance from the people. Demagogues had drawn borders up on maps and told people that lines protected them. In the meantime, Daniel's love showed everybody how insignificant those lines were and how mighty the power of love could be. Juan just started the foundation and it took a life of its own. It was reigned by one principle, love has no borders, neither do parents...

JUAN AND THE PUBIC LICE

Juan was an eighties lover, HIV was still mostly in the gay and iv drug user communities, and he did not protect himself much unless he was doing the prostitution thing to make some money. Needless to say, he contracted everything but HIV. Gonorrhea, Chlamydia, genital warts, herpes, etc. Lucky for Juan, his cousin was a doctor and took care of everything that he got. The herpes was incurable but it was not going to kill him and his cousin gave him the medicine for free. The one scourge that he got from time to time was pubic lice. The first time he got them he did not know he had them. He was living with his auntie and she discovered all these little bloodspots on his underwear. She told him to check himself and he found all these little miniature crabs moving around. He was disgusted. He bought a special shampoo for the lice and shaved all his pubic hair and applied the shampoo. These things really itched on him. He was so glad he got rid of them. A couple of other times he got them again but did not have the money to buy the shampoo, so he would get some roach spray and dilute it in a cup and spread it around his crotch ten minutes before showering. Many years later, while he was incarcerated, he would see the inmates come in with lice infestations and it would remind him of the times when he had to deal with the damn things. In many ways, he believed that bad luck and misery were the real lice in his life, that was before he struck gold with his resort in St. Maarten and all the social work he did. He did not understand that life's trials were like crabs; no matter how hard you tried to get rid off them, you could only do so for a time and inevitably they would come back.

FELO THE SAILOR

Some time after Juan had tried his hand at owning a business and went broke, he decided to go rent a room from his friend Felo, who had been a nuclear submariner for a while and became disabled after being exposed to the radiation of the reactors. You see, they don't tell you that these nuclear reactors leak radiation when you sign up for the Navy, they just hope you don't find out! And Felo found out alright, he started getting old people diseases like crazy. He became bi-polar, developed liver disease, diabetes type 2, eyesight problems. Insomnia, hallucinations, long bouts with depression, you name it, Felo had it. Juan and Felo had become good friends after meeting at a 12 step meeting. Juan had fixed Felo's car a few times and they hung out with friends once in a while. After Juan moving into Felo's house they started to share more time and even started some alternative fuel experiments together to see if they could cash in on saving people fuel. They never materialized but they had a good time together doing them. They worked on cars under Felo's carport whenever Juan would land a job to fix a car. It was pretty cool to see these two hang out. They both liked Linkin, military history, guns, women, adventure, money, they were messy, and were loyal friends. Felo liked his pit bulls and Juan had to adapt to living with big dogs in the house. When Juan was about seven years old he had gotten bitten on the chest by his cousin's German shepherd and it traumatized him about dogs. To this day he will come to my house and ask that the dogs be put away while he is in the house. He will eventually go get them himself and play with them but the initial contact is still traumatic. Oddly enough Juan developed a profound relationship with Felo's pit-bull that lasts to this day.

Felo had an interesting story. He had been an electronics specialist in the service and continued to work in the field after getting out. He traveled the Americas and made decent money but after a while his mental illness got the best of him and could not work any longer. He then decided to start trafficking drugs, namely cocaine and weed. It was work that he found exciting and it did not require many hours, so it was not bad on his bi-polar disorder. He managed to make about a million bucks and buy a couple of houses. Felo pissed away most of his cash on hookers and stuff that he hoarded and never used, but still kept the houses. He was a good friend to have. The night that some morons tried to do a home invasion on Juan's apartment, Juan called Felo and the next day Felo came over to guard Juan with his guns while Juan packed his things. Felo was not a fellow to play with, you did not want to try to hurt him or his friends. Juan eventually moved out into his own apartment but always stayed in contact with Felo, those two will always be friends.

JUAN STARTS A BUSINESS

A few years after Juan had gotten clean he decided to go back to his island and try his luck with a real estate company. Unfortunately for Juan the job never realized and he ended up working for ten bucks an hour under the sun. He had gotten a real estate license to help a friend buy a house and never used it again. As soon as Juan got the license, there were barely any houses available for sale, so Juan had to continue working on cars. A little while after Juan sold his first house the market crashed and banks stopped writing loans. Juan started to believe that he was cursed, everything he went into just went to hell. He never stopped swinging a bat though, not Juan, there was never any quit in him! About a month after Juan was working for his cousin's construction company as a mechanic for ten bucks an hour, his cousin told him that he had a commercial space available and that he would not charge him rent for a few months so he could open a convenience store. Juan was not too crazy about it but still went ahead and took the challenge. It was a brand new building and he had to do all the interior work; steel bars to keep people from breaking in, alarm systems, painting, subcontracting for the a/c systems, procuring shelving, cabinetry, etc. Juan also got a crash course in Puertorican red tape. He had never dealt with such a pile of third world inept hypocrites. Juan refused to bribe any officials for the liquor licenses or the weapons permits. Juan knew he had to pack heat in order to run a cash business in Puerto Rico. You were as good as dead if you didn't. A gun gave you a fighting chance in a place where the crime rate was very high. Juan always kept his wits about him when he was at his store, you never knew when you were going to get robbed. He always kept a stash of about 400 dollars in a bank deposit bag that he kept under the cash register. He had written on it; "for the robbers". Juan decided to open the store without a liquor license, which meant he could not sell beer or any alcohol. It was a big gamble. If you could not sell booze people would not come to the place. That is just the way it is in Puerto Rico. He hired a couple of girls to work part time when he was not there. About two weeks after he opened the store the government had run out of money to pay public employees and contracted services, which left about 300,000 people unemployed in a workforce made of about 1,200,000. It was disastrous for Juan. He had to fire the girls and work the business himself. About four months after he opened it got so bad that he had to start liquidating everything just to eat. His cousin offered to bail him out with some cash loans but Juan did not want to owe anything. The lady from the alcohol bureau showed almost five months after Juan had applied for the liquor license, only to deny him the license. Juan called them all kinds of names and swore he would sue them for discrimination. The reason they did not grant him the license was that an evangelical school for profit was close to Juan's store and the hypocrite pastor who ran it had complained about it to the authorities. So funny how people profit enormously from religion and they won't let others make a living. I think if Jesus walked the earth today he would torch a lot of "Christian" organization's buildings. Juan finally liquidated his assets and recovered a little of his investment. He had lost about 50 thousand dollars in his little adventure following his cousin's advise. He was hurt and now only had less than ten grand to start over after losing almost all his life's savings. It was hard for him to swallow, but he had to. You see, Juan's prayer was: "God, if you exist, what are you training me for", and would then say; "fuck you man", with his middle finger pointed at heaven and a big, warm, loving smile and a chuckle. He would take many of the lessons from establishing his store and apply them to the rest of his life. It was a financial failure, and Juan understood that the best teacher is failure, he just wished he could get out of her classroom.

JUAN GRADUATES FROM COLLEGE

Years after Juan got clean and sober he found himself heartbroken, broke, divorced, and facing another crossroads in his life. He decided to go and finish his college degree. He only needed twelve credits to do so. So he got on a plane and went to live with his grandma for a semester. Juan had been living in the states for a long time now and was not used to the lifestyle of his island any longer. The first day back he was watching the news and saw this young man lying on the pavement next to his car, where he had been gunned down. He was still taking breaths but no one was coming to help him, even though there were hundreds of people around, including the police and paramedics. When a reporter from one of the TV stations started asking one of the paramedics why they wouldn't help, the paramedic answered that the guy was already dead but was gasping. Juan almost wanted to drive over there and save this guy and slap all the cops and paramedics for letting him die. It later surfaced why they wouldn't help him. The gunmen had called the police and issued a warning that said they would kill anyone who tried to save the guy. It was disgusting to Juan to see his countrymen succumb to the fear of such pieces of shit. Juan was bred to fight for the needy, to help the people. It was like he had woken up in the planet of the apes and everybody was a coward. And on top of that, nobody cared. Right away Juan knew that he had changed inside, that one of the reasons he got high and drunk was to tame the pain of such awful inhumanity amongst humans.

Juan talked to his friend the doctor and rented his old car. He had to fix a bunch of stuff but it still ran. It also happened to be the same type of car that Lucía had when she was going to college, so it didn't matter to Juan that it was all beat up because it reminded him of her. Juan stayed with his grandmother, in an old subdivision between two of the worst projects of the island. One of them was where his cousin used to live but he was too busy with school to visit. This time his grandmother gave him a key to the house and Juan was trusted again. He felt like he was part of the family again. His grandma would cook for him everyday and watch him study on the dinner table before class. It was very peaceful for both of them. Juan would go to the beach and ride his boogie board almost every day and then go to school. Most of the classes he breezed through, they were easy for him since he had a business minded thinking process. He met a couple of good looking women at school and bagged a few of them a couple of times, always the player. Juan never stopped thinking about Lucía though, he wondered if she was living in Puerto Rico. After Juan finished taking his last final test, he booked a plane ticket to Florida for the next day. The social decomposition in Puerto Rico was about to drive him crazy and he could not take it anymore. His stepdad offered to finance an auto repair shop for him, but he declined, he just wanted to get away from all the social upheaval in his island. The funny thing is that he had gotten off his anti-depressants while he was in Puerto Rico but had to get back on them as soon as he got to Florida because he started having panic attacks. One big accomplishment for Juan was to buy a house for his auntie and Carlos because they had no house of their own. He was finally able to give something to his beloved mother's sister, Juan felt on top of the world for having done that. When Juan finished taking his last test he knew he had accomplished an important personal goal, to finish his bachelor's degree. He went to the cemetery where his mother was buried and sobbed on his knees in front of her tomb and looked up into the sky and screamed: "I did it Mom, I did it, this one's for you Mami!".

JUAN SCREAMS AT GOD

On a trip with his beloved wife Lucía Juan was sitting in the passenger side of their 1967 impala four door. They were listening to music from 10 cc, the windows were down and the cold crisp air in the upper 50's was coming in and bathing them in a kind of delicious coat of heaven, with the full moon piercing the clouds with its rays. It was just Juan and Lucía, and they always dreamed of this moment when they could enjoy a long drive down a state road in the south, far away from home and right inside each other's love. Juan told Lucía to pull over on top of an overpass by a small town just so he could kiss her passionately and delicately and give her all his soul in one kiss. It seemed to stop time, that kiss did. They felt each other's heartbeats, every particle of life inside their breaths as they shared the air. They looked inside their brown eyes, really deep, in peace, in awe, in oneness. Time would not move, each blink holding infinity inside of it. Their hands caressing each other's faces, the tips of their fingers painting on their cheeks. Drawing invisible and eternal hearts with their names written side by side. Like an unspoken, unsolicited promise of eternity as one soul, being signed in front of God. Caressing one face with the other, smelling eternity with every breath of heaven, falling deep in every direction, timelessness, abandon, peace, light, electricity, hahhhh..... the universe panting in ecstasy in the presence of this love. Juan and Lucía had given life to everything with that moment, with their love given to its owners they had become immortal, givers of the essence that gives life to all...

They kissed and were never done. Going down the road Juan remembered that he was meaning to scream at God about having to die, but after the kiss he understood that love is God and theirs was eternal, they were never going to die, they would live forever in the kisses of lovers and romantics, in the hugs of fire between enamored souls who surrendered to love in the middle of hopelessness and hope.

JUAN'S FRIEND MANOLO

When Juan went to get help at a twelve step fellowship he really struggled identifying with some of these people. They were not hardcore enough. These people had jobs, houses, cars, and families. Juan had been a street dope fiend. He was not raised like that but he ended up where he could not hold a job, have a family, money, or have anything of value without selling it for drugs. Juan kept going back to using drugs and would come back to the meetings to pick up another white key chain as a symbol of another try at staying clean. The one thing that kept happening though, was that Juan did not like the emotional pain he experienced every time he fucked up. He was tired. He would hire a prostitute and did not want to do her because he saw his pain in her. It was some type of spiritual experience that was going on inside of him. Or maybe he was growing up. Juan knew he wanted more out of life, peace, freedom, not slavery. He had started trying to quit drugs at twenty four, the age he always thought would be his death year. Finally, after being tired and beat up emotionally, he found a guy who understood him and started to help him work on his problems. The guy was Manolo. He was a former ex-con, ex-junkie from Brooklyn, who had spent almost 25 years in prison for different crimes. He had lived it all, homelessness, being shot at, stabbed, gangs, robbery, burglaries, homicides, drug dealing, the works. Most of Manolo's children were born in penitentiaries to his gangster wives. He had tested positive to HIV twice and then tested negative twice, had Hep-c, emphysema, you name it, he had it. But the most important thing he had was understanding and love. Manolo had been saved from the clutches of death by the love of his family. The last time he got out of prison he went right back to doing heroin and methadone. By the time his family did an intervention on him he was doing 10 bags of heroin and 100mg of methadone a day. He almost died in the withdrawal process. His arms were destroyed with abscesses and puss. He had to wrap them in gauze for a few months and wear long sleeve shirts so as not to upset people. When Juan asked Manolo to help him, Manolo gladly accepted and they started to work together. Manolo told Juan to write down everything he did the last time he got high, so Juan did and they both discussed what Juan had written in the yellow legal pad paper. Juan thought Manolo was going to tell him to burn the paper afterwards but he didn't. Manolo told him to fold it and keep it in his wallet and read it every time he felt like drinking or drugging again. At the beginning of Juan's journey out of addiction county, Juan would need to read the whole thing to get spooked into staying clean. After a few months, just opening his wallet and seeing the yellow paper in there was enough. Manolo started guiding Juan through the process of self improvement and Juan was willing because Manolo never judged him. Even though Juan did not understand and disagreed with some of the questions in the literature of the twelve step program he was using for help, Manolo made him understand that all he needed to do was use whatever he needed to get better. For eleven years Juan was willing to overlook the flaws of the twelve step program he went to, and life for him was ok. But something kept burning inside of him, something that told him that he was not done evolving yet. That is the subject of another chapter though, back to Manolo. Manolo had been a paratrooper with the eighty second airborne division and never got Brooklyn out of his blood. One time Manolo jumped in the jungle in Panama as part of a mission and decided to do some hustling with the natives of the jungle. He offered his spare pair of boots in exchange for some weed. About a half an hour later these Indians come back with a duffel bag full of prime choice Panamanian marihuana. Manolo also raided the first aid kits from the military airplanes for the morphine doses. Miraculously Manolo made it out of the army with an honorable discharge. It was all downhill from there for Manolo. Life in Brooklyn as a street hustling dope fiend was no walk in the park. Manolo told Juan his stories and Juan really felt comfortable and identified with him. Everything from sticking a forty five caliber pistol in the milkman's face every morning, to transporting large amounts of cash in luggage bags. Manolo used to get sent to Attica on a frequent basis, he even participated in the infamous riots of the seventies. He told Juan how he was digging holes in the yard looking for a stash of heroin he had buried, while the rest of the prison was in full riot. He was such a hardcore dope fiend that the government sent him to a federal hospital where they did experiments on him to understand addiction. Manolo always spoke of an experiment where he was sent to a Kentucky federal prison. They had young doctors feeding heroin to a monkey in a cage. After the monkey had gotten hooked on the heroin, they let the monkey withdraw cold turkey. Some time after the monkey was healthy, the doctors put some heroin in a corner of the cage where the monkey was. The monkey broke his neck, literally, trying to get out of the cage and away from the heroin. When Manolo saw that he asked himself; "what the fuck is wrong with me?", because no matter how hard the drugs had made him suffer, he would always go back to them. Many times, while being in prison, Manolo would get his mother to go cop for him and bring the dope to him in prison. She would have to go and catch a bus and take a very long ride to upstate New York prisons, just so that her son would not have to withdraw. Manolo would take the drugs and sell some of them to the other inmates. He walked out of prison one time with fifteen thousand dollars as a product of his hustling in the joint. His last bid was ten to life. He had tested positive for HIV and was really depressed about it. Manolo would get up in the morning and put his pistol in the dope dealer's mouth, steal all the dealer's money, dope, and jewelry, go get off, and come back to the park and sit right in front of the dealer he just robbed to see if he would try something. He did not give a flying fuck, period!

Manolo's family had bought him a ticket to Florida as a last ditch attempt to get him to quit drugs. He was still withdrawing from 100 mg of methadone and one bundle of heroin a day. He was also using Xanax and they had weaned him off in seven days in a clinic in New York. He was in hell. His arms had open sores and abscesses all over. He was injecting himself through the jugular vein because that was the only place he could find a vein. In prison he would use sharpened basketball filler needles to inject himself, so, needless to say, his arms were a mess. He would squeeze his arms and pus and blood would come out. His first thirty days clean were horrible, he could only sleep inside his sister's car while she drove around the neighborhood, and only for fleeting moments. She would drive him around every night after she took him to a twelve step meeting. At first, he went to the meetings to see if someone would take him to cop, but slowly he started to get better. A lot of people shunned him because there are always hypocrites in the world. Everybody was scared of his abscesses and his HIV. But in the middle of the fear there were a couple of people who were brave enough to love him unconditionally. They told him that he did not have to use drugs anymore and that there was another life he could live, one without slavery. I guess he believed them because he stayed clean for almost twenty years, when he died of cancer in a ravaged liver. It turned out that Manolo was not HIV positive. They did two more tests on him after he had cleaned up and he tested negative. To be sure, Manolo went to the best HIV hospital in the country and the doctors there did all the tests necessary and found him to be free of HIV. Apparently Manolo was one of the humans who carry the CCR5 DELTA 32 mutation that makes them immune to HIV. Before death, he saved countless lives, including Juan's. This almost did not happen though. Manolo almost left because he could not identify with the people at the meetings. They talked about jobs, but the only job he ever had was pressing license plates in the joint. People talked about having houses, but Manolo only knew about the cardboard condominiums he built for himself under the Brooklyn bridge. People talked about eating lobster, but the closest he came to that was the cat food he ate while telling himself it was pâté. Whenever people tried to mention specific drugs or started talking about the raw experiences they had had as a result of their addiction, they were admonished. It wasn't until Manolo went to a 12 step convention that he heard a speaker talk about putting balloons filled with drugs in his rectum, to be able to introduce them to the prison, that Manolo knew there were others like him and that it was OK to stick around amongst these very weird hypocritical people. There were some good people among them and that alone was worth the effort. Juan named his second son Manolo in honor of his friend who saved his life. He also paid for the last vacation that Manolo took. He did not want to go to Disney world, he just wanted to walk around his old neighborhood and play dominoes with the old people from the bodega. He wanted to go to Coney Island, and ride over the Brooklyn Bridge, to look at the Hudson one more time, and to walk Manhattan on a Sunday afternoon. Juan paid for all of it and said goodbye to his friend who saved his life and gave him the opportunity to give life to others, just like he did with Juan. Long live Manolo's soul, BRAVA...!!!

JUAN GETS HIS HEART BROKEN AND UNBROKEN

Juan was comfortable in his marriage, he had a few cars, a race car, a little business, a house with his wife, and there was no pain in his heart. He thought that was happiness. But the truth was that he never stopped loving Lucía and that every day he thought of her just a little, and sometimes a lot. He remembered how one time at a bar he was talking to a guy and the man asked him what he was thinking about. He told him he was thinking about Lucía. The man at the bar asked him if he loved her and Juan said he did with all his heart. The man then told Juan to go and look for her and don't look back. His life had become bland; he was never in love with his wife even though he appreciated her and what she had done for him as a person. He knew inside his heart that he had to see his Lucía one more time before he died, he prayed for her, and even sent her happy birthday wishes through the air on her birthday. Juan had lost Lucía for the first time when she went off to college. He could not follow her because of his raging cocaine and alcohol addiction. Lucía had become a casualty of his demons. He never forgot how hard and deep it hurt when they said goodbye at his apartment. It was like someone had reached inside his pericardium and installed needles that poked his heart every time it beat.

About 6 and a half years into his marriage Juan got a phone call from María, a mutual friend of Lucía and him. María's brother was getting married and she wanted to see Juan and hang out. Lucía was also going to be at the wedding, so Juan did everything in his power to go alone. He wanted to see how he felt when seeing her, it was a question that he needed answered and boy did he ever find out! When at the wedding Juan and Lucía hung out together. Lucía was halfway through a pregnancy and her hair was not combed thoroughly. Juan knew it then like he always knew, he had never stopped loving her and never would. He did not hesitate to tell her either. He waited until there was a moment of privacy and just told her while looking deep into her eyes. Lucía looked so sad before Juan told her of his love for her. It was like she was a prisoner of something. She could not muster a full smile or light up her aura like she used to. Juan later learned that she was entangled with an abusive man with whom she was having a third child. Juan was screwed, he was married, broke, and he knew he was going to leave his wife to get together with Lucía, kids, no kids, man, or no man, it was on. They dated a little after her son was born and it seemed like things were going to be good, but it was not to be. After Juan had spent almost ten grand getting Lucía an apartment, a car, paying off her debts, getting her a live in nanny, and paying for a Disney vacation, Lucía returned to her abusive husband and Juan was destroyed. Juan felt betrayed, spat on, stabbed in the back, but above all his heart was destroyed. He never loved anyone like his Lucía, nobody had reached so deep into his soul. Juan had walked into the apartment that he had gotten Lucía and her children and the other guy was there lounging and Lucía was wearing a bath robe. He talked to the guy and believed all the lies he told him so Juan turned around and left full of pain and anger. He told a few choice insults to Lucía and proceeded to leave with a boatload of pain in his soul. Later on Juan asked Lucía to at least return the money he paid for the apartment so that he did not feel like a fool paying for an apartment for the guy to live in. She told him that since he had called her a whore that was what she had charged him to sleep with him. Many years later Juan had learned the truth about battered women syndrome and how it rendered women almost helpless against their aggressors. But the knowledge did not take away his anger, he never understood how someone could be so evil towards good people and so nice to those who hurt them. He learned about battered woman syndrome from Lucía when they ran into each other again. This time she had conquered a lot of her demons and had bettered herself in many areas. Not like Juan cared about her defects, he loved her still and told her again in her face, like only he could do. They cried and talked, and kissed and hugged and apologized to each other, and loved each other with all their clothes on. Lucía told Juan how she had escaped from the guy and went to live to Central America for a while with her boys. She explained to Juan how she had to let him go because if she had not, one of them was going to end up dead or in jail. She knew Juan could handle himself and the father of her boys would not stop threatening her. It was a recipe for disaster and Juan understood it many years later. It still bothered Juan though, the fact that there were so many years lost where he knew he still loved Lucía and they had not been together. It also bothered Juan that Lucía never admitted to any wrongdoing and blamed the breakup on Juan because of the way he reacted. She thought she was saving Juan from an explosive deadly situation by getting rid of him and allowing her ex into her life. Juan hated that she still manipulated the truth but chose to ignore it. I guess when two souls love each other so deeply, all they have to do is allow themselves to tell each other the truth about their feelings and their love will show them the way. Nowadays Juan tells me that he and Lucía laughed about it in their little cabin in the Appalachian mountains when they went for a vacation. It was part of a very intense learning process that showed them what really mattered in life. When they kissed, they kissed forever, when they laughed, the earth shook, when they made love, stars were born. But there would be one more breakup before these two finally let life take its course. You see, Lucía never loved Juan as deeply as Juan loved her and Juan hated that she could not be completely honest about their last breakup. She never allowed herself to completely fall. Juan knew it and he overlooked it and it came back to bite him. Knowing that something is going to happen does not take the pain away when it happens, it just gets you on guard and exhausts you emotionally and physically. Juan saw that Lucia never had loyalty towards him. She saw him as a friend with benefits. She turned on the love and the charm when they were together and then switched it back off when Juan went away to his place. She never really had any intentions of forging a life with him, Juan was just fun to her, nothing more. That hurt Juan's feelings. Here was this guy who was the quintessential friend with benefits, but could not do it with Lucía because he loved her. Many years later, when Juan was with María in St. Maarten, Lucía came and visited and Juan let her stay in one the huts of his resort. María knew about Lucía but she did not care, she knew Juan loved Lucía. She even taunted Lucía telling her how stupid she was for leaving such a great guy. They became kind of friends though. María even suggested that they do a manage au trois if Juan wanted. They did, and Lucía fell in love with Juan this time and had become an honest person after a lifetime of being scared of it. She decided to stay in St. Maarten and work as a marketing and advertising consultant for Juan and María. The three had a great time and neither María nor Lucía were bothered by the unusual relationship they established. They were the dream team of hospitality and business networking in the Caribbean, the three musketeers. Juan had never experienced the Pasha life, with these two women tending to his gifted brain and implementing his vision of a family in business, instead of the predatory tactics that prevailed in the business world. They were envied, feared, but most of all, loved by those they did business with. Their vision of peaceful co-existence brought a new type of clientele to their resort. The super wealthy, super liberal, and super peaceful visionaries of the world, all came to Juan's resort in St. Maarten.

JUAN GOES TO WAR
AGAINST 12 STEP FELLOWSHIPS

Juan had been a good follower for a long time but one day something inside of him broke after he saw a beautiful young woman get chased out of an NA meeting under threat of bodily harm. This girl had been dating a couple of the guys from the group and the "spiritual" and "recovered addicts" had mounted a character assassination campaign against her, complete with "you whore" text messages, threatening phone calls, and all kinds of direct and indirect shunning. The NA spiritual gurus, led by a former gangster, murderer, child kidnapper, and now spiritual leader of the group, had written and implemented rules to discourage dating amongst heterosexual members of NA. They even suggested segregated fellowshipping amongst men and women at the beginning of every meeting and called people who dated before their first year clean, sexual predators. Something had to be done, thought Juan. This was not right. People had to respect people's freedoms, not condemn them for exercising them. Juan and his friend Shane had to escort that girl into her car to protect her from the lynch mob. It was surreal, here were all these retired (most of them at least) prostitutes, murderers, thieves, robbers, scam artists, kidnappers, and deadbeat parents who pimped out their daughters for a 20 dollar hit of crack, bullying a defenseless young woman for exercising her birthright of seeking affectionate companionship. The girl went home and ate 15 Percocets in one sitting before Juan could talk to her the next day on the phone. She survived, thank God thought Juan. The one thing that did not survive was Juan's idleness on the matter. He went on line and blasted all the perpetrators of the offense. He wrote to People who control the NA fellowship, but to no avail. They actually washed their hands off. The more he started trying to raise awareness about the issue of bullying based on the exercise of constitutional freedoms, the more he encountered people who supported it. It was insane. It was the one tool that many of these very sick hypocritical people preferred to use to make themselves feel better about the horrors they had caused to society and their families. Juan could not believe it; it was like everything he heard about unconditional love and open mindedness in the NA fellowship was a lie. Those who supported his ideas did so in a very quiet non supportive way. It was like he woke up in the southern US one morning and it was 1950, only this was the 21st century and the heterosexual people were the prosecuted. The people who were in charge of the place where the group met, were trespassing people who confronted them about their abuses of power and some had even been physically attacked for confronting the bullying. The rest of the group went along with the abuse or sided with the bullies because it suited their need to feel better by abusing others. A couple of Juan's best friends also got trespassed from the group's premises for cursing out the bullies. Juan confronted the bullies in group meetings but nothing got done about it, so he decided to change fellowships and go to AA meetings. There, he ran into very stern opposition every time he said he was an addict, some groups even asked him to leave because they did not want addicts in their meetings! Never mind that alcoholism is alcohol addiction and that alcohol is the most damaging drug of all. He found out that alcoholics thought of themselves as better than people addicted to illegal street drugs and that they did not want to be associated with them because it damaged their reputation. Their excuse was that the person looking to get help from alcoholism would be turned away if they learned of the presence of junkies in the premises. Juan was fuming about this whole thing. He had given over ten years of his life to encouraging recovery through the use of 12 step programs and now had discovered their dark sides. He was heart broken, disturbed, and felt abandoned. All his circle of friends had been built from the fellowships and he now knew he had to walk away from the farce of 12 step programs. He thought about drinking, smoking weed, doing some coke, and then thought about fighting these bastards from within with the best weapon of all, the truth. He knew it was going to be an uphill battle, but he also knew that in the process he was going to learn how to address his explosive and passionate emotions about people who abuse others. He knew that this was a pivotal fight that he could not choose to withdraw from if he wanted to grow into an effective communicator and achieve his dream of becoming a great man. Juan believed that, just like Dr. King had said, "everybody can be great because everybody can serve". This realization did not come cheap. He spent many sleepless nights festering about the abuses and the possibility of many people being harmed by those who were supposed to help them. Poor Juan, he still believed that someday humanity would care about humans. I respected him so much for that. Juan decided to contact other groups to see if the practice was widespread, and it was. It was also accepted. It was an acceptable collateral damage. At the beginning he withdrew from both fellowships and just went to school and visited his son. He really really did not have time for the bullshit, but somewhere inside he knew that he had to do something for the people who were getting kicked out of 12 step programs. People with addiction problems were the lepers of the twentieth century and he did not want them to continue to be treated like that in the 21st century or ever. After the two years had passed he went back to see some of his friends and found that some people were now understanding what he was saying about not leaving anybody behind by bullying them out of a place that is supposed to help them. Some were now siding against the bullies. But the bullying was still going on, and always against the weak and disenfranchised, mainly homeless, weak spirited, mentally ill, heterosexual people. The same groups that were disenfranchised in mainstream society were abused in 12 step fellowships. Juan found it stupid to see a bunch of weeds trying to get rid of the weeds. HA!, the stupidity of classism. When it came to helping people Juan had one rule; noone gets left behind, NOONE!

JUAN'S FRIEND IRISH TIM

Juan had the talent of attracting some really sick individuals and loving them unconditionally and with tough love. Irish Tim was a washed up Wall Street investment manager who had lost it all through a bad marriage to a high class hooker with a bad cocaine habit. He was no saint though, this guy could do some serious drugging and partying without any help whatsoever. Two can piss away more money than one, that's for sure. He was making close to 20 grand a month in investment returns in his early forties and was pretty much retired before this woman came into his life. When she came into the picture she pretty much took care of that right away though. These two should have never gotten together though, they were USDA prime choice liars, liked cocaine too much, and could manipulate better than anybody in their neighborhoods. Irish Tim came from an upper middle class New York family with ties to manufacturing, his father had invented Teflon and gotten his idea stolen by DuPont and never cashed in on it. While growing up he had been rebellious and wild. Him and his brother were running large amounts of marihuana and cocaine by the time they were seventeen and eighteen. They went to college and graduated with business and finance degrees and Tim went to work for a Wall Street investment firm in his early twenties. He was doing fine but knew that he needed to work for himself, he was born to be an entrepreneur, so he quit his job and started a construction firm. At one time he had twenty seven crews working full time across the eastern United States. This is when he met the soon to be mother of his child. He had decided to get some help for his addiction problem and checked into a rehab facility. That did not last long because while in treatment in Louisiana he saw a hotel being built right next door to the treatment place and saw the opportunity to bid for the construction crews and got it. So he ended up leaving treatment and building the hotel and making a ton of money. He did continue to go to AA meetings when he returned to Florida, where he met his soon to be wife. He was in love and they were soon married and pregnant. Before she got pregnant they were going through ten grand a week in drugs and parties for about a year. They had also bought a house cash and started to work on the retirement money really fast. They stopped when she got pregnant and he went back to work as a general contractor. It was not long before she had the baby and they were both hard at partying. They ended up pissing it all away inside a crack pipe and a whiskey bottle and both having to live in people's couches. She kept the baby girl for a while but could not stop doing drugs to save her life. Tim was homeless but kept trying to make a living as a handyman and sometimes a con man. Once in a while he would collect money from a customer as a down payment on a job and disappear and move to another county. He would try to get clean again by going to NA meetings and would succeed for a little while and fall back on his face. That's when he met Juan. Juan found the guy funny and full of shit at the same time. I guess that Juan got a kick out of how many lies per minute this guy could tell with a straight face and a deep voice. It was downright entertaining. When Juan learned that Tim was homeless he offered to rent him a room in his three bedroom duplex house. Juan knew Tim could not pay him until he made some money from his handyman gig. It was cool with him though. Tim had his little six year old girl with him and Juan was not going to let them sleep out in the cold. Juan had to teach Tim not to bullshit and lie to him about not having the rent money. Juan taught Tim that the first thing you secure is a roof and a meal for your kid and the rest was high class bullshit. It was not easy though, Juan had to get on Tim's face quite often to make him understand. One time Tim came home high and Juan knew it but let him slide on it. Tim also kept bringing home all sorts of stuff he found on the side of the road, broken radios, TV sets, furniture, helicopter parts, you name it, this guy brought it home and stored it. Juan had to stop him before he turned the place into a dump. Tim would also bring home his work crew, which was mostly made up of homeless people he found at twelve step meetings. He wanted to move them all in so he could secure his labor for his business. Juan would not have any of it though. He rented the other room to one of the workers but kicked him out really quick when he found out the guy's girlfriend was way underage and the guy had a problem with stealing. Tim tried to move his sister in with him but Juan again turned him down and told him to stop fucking with him or he was going to kick him and his daughter out. Juan had had it with Tim's manipulative and conniving ways and he let him know. Eventually Tim moved out into an apartment with his ex and his daughter. It was next to Juan's and it was kind of a relief for Juan. He really did not appreciate all the craziness in his life when Tim was in the house. It was a lifestyle that he had been done with a long time ago and it made some bad memories return when he saw Tim living it. Juan learned a lesson in patience, tolerance and compassion by letting Tim live with him though. It was like training a wild horse to let someone ride it again. Juan saw in Tim all the bad habits he was done with after he cleaned up his act. I guess when people see all their defects manifested in others it really bothers them, regardless of whether they do them anymore or not. Humanity has a knack for hypocrisy, specially when they have insecurity issues like Juan did. Juan despised hypocrites though. It was like a switch went on when he dealt with them. He could not stand hypocrisy because it had hurt him so much. If he could only understand that we all have a little bit of hypocrisy in us he would not have suffered so much. I guess one has to learn to accept others with their faults and know when to draw the line. That's something Juan had not figured out yet but would in the future. It took him a lot of tears and Pepto Bismol, but most of all , love.

Irish Tim moved to the west coast after learning he had developed a degenerative nerve disease. The weather was better for him over there. He stayed in contact with Juan all the time and when he returned to Florida he met up with him. Tim was homeless again and had relinquished custody of his little girl to the mother. She was staying clean and sober with the help of the court system with a probation paper and a breathalyzer device to help her start her car. Tim had gotten his disability approved but it was a miserly six hundred dollars a month. It did not bother him though. He seemed happy and carefree. He knew he was living on borrowed time anyway. They had found four aneurisms in his brain when they were doing his diagnoses in the hospital. Juan always told him to not push when he pooped, because it could pop his aneurisms. Eventually Tim found a paid research trial for his nerve disorder and he was able to get an apartment and a Truck with the money he got. When he lost his apartment Tim moved into his truck and even fitted it with a house air conditioning unit because it would have been too expensive to fix the truck's a/c system. He even installed a generator to power the a/c. Tim eventually settled down with filthy rich old woman who fell in love with him after he did some repairs on her house. Juan was always teasing Tim about having granny sex. He would ask Tim "you fucking her yet?" and Tim would always reply the same; "fuck you!". It was comical to see these two in action. Juan and Tim really loved each other, no matter what. Juan always told me that if he ever hit the lotto he would buy a big property with acreage and stick Tim in a little guest house to tend to the cows and shit. I think Tim and Juan would have made quite the comedy team. One time Tim and Juan went to a Hollywood Video store and Tim let out this humongous fart, I mean, the store shook! Juan started laughing uncontrollably and landed face first on the ground of the store. He could barely get back on his feet. Meanwhile Tim, in the back of the store, kept looking behind him to see if there were any children behind. He was afraid he had hurt someone with that thing being so loud and all. It was something they never forgot. Years later, while Juan and Tim got together with a couple of other friends at a pizza joint, they still talked about the fart that almost killed them both. By that time Tim had progressed in his insanity and was telling everybody stories about being abducted by aliens and the grays. He had become a full blown alien, asteroid, Mayan end of days prophecies, orb watching freak. Juan loved him even more for his craziness. Not to mention that Juan also believed, or wanted to believe, in crypto zoology, aliens, and stuff. He really wished he could see and hang out with Sasquatch before he died. Juan really didn't think Tim was crazy, he knew Tim was playing with people's heads when he acted like an alien freak. It gave him attention and mysticism. Tim liked to play the drums, specially the congas. They always talked about getting together to play but never did. There was a sadness inside of Juan because he could never spend enough time with his friend Tim. Juan wished he had met Tim back in the old days when Tim was doing better both physically and mentally. But in a way he knew that Tim was finally free, finally loved life more than anything else, and that gave Juan some relief. Juan wished he could have all his friends close by and live in peace and harmony. He had seen so many of his close friends die and live in such horrible scenarios. That tended to depress and hurt him. Juan was deeply sentimental about his friends and never wanted any of them to go through all the pain they went through. It was Juan's life, these were his lemons that had rained from heaven on him and all around him. The depth of Juan's love for Tim was immense, indescribable, insufferable, an immovable force of the universe that gives life to all......

Last I heard, Juan and Tim had started a joint venture doing custom cabinets for wealthy people. They always argued and fought, and eventually reached agreements that benefited only Tim, and Juan was ok with that, he really just wanted to see Tim own his own little place outright before Tim died. Tim kept inviting Juan to play his congas with the homeless people at the park and Juan kept blowing him off, but then decided to go and had some serious fun. Other than the cops kicking them out for hanging out with the homeless, everything was cool. Orlando had a bad reputation as a Gestapo for the homeless. The mayor even passed an ordinance banning the feeding of homeless humans in public places. You could feed all the dogs you wanted, you just could not feed the public in public places. Juan started hanging out with Tim a little more after that, Juan knew that at any moment one of those aneurisms could rupture and that would be it. Not yet, not yet though, Juan thought, not yet. Tim sold his business for millions and lived in peace with his congas and his son on weekends. He would travel to Juan's place in the Caribbean a couple of times a year and counsel guests in matters of spirituality and life's meaning, nothing like a reformed bullshit artist to restore faith in humanity...

JUAN'S CURSE

Juan always knew he should have gone to law school when he was younger. It was too late now though. He was in his forties, with a small child, no money, his health failing him, and with no desire to acquire 200 thousand dollars in extra student loans on top of the 40 he already had. Juan was tired of fighting and losing, and only having the scars to show for, while the rest of his childhood friends from his catholic school days had successful financial and personal lives. He saw all the abuses perpetrated against him and humanity by the governments and other people. It's like Juan could see things that were hurting people that the people themselves could not see. It was his curse; his eyes had been opened to all the nastiness that mankind does to one another. He wished he did not see it. At times he just wanted to be like those people who just existed and were happy with whatever little crumbs their masters fed them. But the education bug still poked at him. Juan was a natural advocate, a thinker, a true analyst of people and their motives. He knew he was born to champion lost causes, the type that whole nations gave up on. He was a fire starter and a social conscience agitator. He still had a glimmer of hope that somehow he would become a lawyer and help the abused. He just wished the path there was not so uncertain. He had a misdemeanor battery conviction, no experience as a lawyer, no money, would have to go deeply into depth, and suffered from bouts of crippling depression, breathlessness, stomach problems, and on and on. He had lost so many times that he was emotionally worn out, he had lost faith in society, in most humans. He was scared to go for anything anymore for the fear of losing again and being stuck with the bill. He was also scared that he would regret not going for broke when he could. Middle age is a motherfucker! He wished he did not have any more regrets, that he could just settle into something that paid good money and that he loved. So far, no cigar for Juan. He was not fighting his demons of insecurity and guilt. He was scared of pain because it had been such a daily thing for him. I guess you could say he had a mix of ADD, and PTSD, it must have not been easy being Juan in those days. People criticized him for attempting so many things in his forties and not going for one in particular, but they forgot that he had squandered about eleven years of his life on drugs and alcohol, so, technically, he was in his twenties, when most people are experimenting with life's options. People judge so much, and then when someone makes a big contribution they say; "I knew he was meant for greatness". Good thing Juan was stubborn and made his own path. Although he did not know it then, all the trials and tribulations he went through would make Juan a force to be reckoned with in the field of business development, marketing, advertising, and strategic analysis. He read up on law books for sport and decided on not going to law school. He did not need it, his resort and business venture investments paid off big and left him residuals for life. He invested in a friend's sandwich company and it went through the roof. His friend sold half of the company to facebook when the company started diversifying and the rest is history. Juan is a silent partner and just counts the money from his returns. So, you see, Juan's uncertainty as to what he was going to do when he grew up was not uncertainty all. He got his fingers into many pies and some of them sold very well and still do so. He would always tell me; "Ray, you gotta swing and keep swinging; eventually you're going to hit something out of the park". Juan wasn't lying...

JUAN'S AUNTIE MARY

Juan's mother's sister was his favorite person in the world. She was a "jabá", which means a person with Caucasian features and African hair. She was a cosmetologist along with Juan's mother and they were very close beloved sisters. Ever since she was young she was vivacious with a contagious laugh. She married her college sweetheart and they had a boy named Carlos. During the c- section the doctor took too long to get the boy out and he lost oxygen to his brain, which caused severe developmental and brain injuries that would not be evident until the baby was about 2 years old. Mary's husband was an economist in the cabinet of the island's governor. He left Mary when Carlos was 5 because he was ashamed of having a handicapped son and he had also found a woman besides Juan's auntie. She was devastated and furious but she used all that rage to fight for Carlos' rights. Carlos needed neurologists, physical therapists, speech therapists, etc. The problem was that in Juan's island the infrastructure for helping handicapped people was lacking to say the least. Mary became the champion of handicapped children's rights in the island. She marched on the capitol, the executive mansion, organized action committees, volunteered for fund raising events, educated parents new to the handicap world and just flat out became a champion of the handicapped in the island. Mary adored her nephew Juan.

When Juan's mother died she was there and was watching her sister's body through a glass in the room where her body was laying on a table after they removed all the machines from her. Mary saw her sister open her eyes and smile at her and she spoke to her telepathically and told her to take care of Juan for her. They were both mediums and could talk to angels and the spirits of the dead. Not at will, but they could influence outcomes of situations when it came to their children. Carlos had inherited his mother's special touch but his manifested in the ability to feel what people around him were feeling, even if they were not showing it. Juan believed Carlos was an angel in the body of a handicapped human. Even though he could not talk or walk, he could detect the presence of pain, sorrow, or evil in somebody before anybody else could. Carlos and Juan always were the closest of cousins. Juan knew how to feed Carlos without making him choke. Carlos did not have the ability to chew like normal people and pretty much swallowed his food almost whole. Carlos also had epilepsy and had to take tegretol, which dried up the mucus in his gastro intestinal tract and gave him chronic severe constipation. For thirty five years Mary had to use all kinds of methods to make Carlos have bowel movements. If she didn't he would go over a week without it and end up in the hospital. It was a constant struggle to keep Carlos alive but he was Mary's pride and joy, her angel. Mary would always keep a space for Juan wherever she was living since he was living like a Gipsy. Juan would stay at Mary's whenever he would need a place to stay and rest after a long binge on the streets or whenever he was hungry and tired. She was always there for him and was the one who prompted Juan to get help for his addiction problem. Juan bought her a little house in the country so that she could be in peace with Carlos. She had dedicated her life to caring for Carlos and had to live with very little money, since Carlos' father only paid her child support once in a while. It was OK though, Juan would later take care of his auntie and Carlos with all his might. After he found financial success he bought her a nicer house in Puerto Rico and a vacation apartment in Florida. He got her a handicap van to drive around and a paid assistant to help her handle Carlos. Before Carlos died at the age of 40 Juan was able to give him the best care available and as much entertainment as he could handle. Carlos kissed Juan on the cheek minutes before passing and laughed hard with a sparkle in his eyes. They buried Carlos with Juan's mother because they loved each other so much. After Carlos' passing Juan's auntie went to live with him part time and would counsel parents who were new to having a handicapped child. She was very experienced and always lent a helping hand to anyone who needed it. She also had talent with make up because she had studied it before dedicating her life to caring for Carlos. Many people would want to get married in Juan's resort and she would fly in to do the make up. She would not charge the people anything, she just wanted Juan to succeed. Always taking care of Juan, forever...

JUAN'S UNCLE, LITO

Juan's mother had a little brother who she loved dearly. He was the youngest of four, two girls and two boys. Juan's grandma had married his grandpa and they had moved to New York for work. They had their first boy in their island and the rest in New York. Juan's grandpa was a very bright, autodidact, who never went past the second grade in elementary school and had taught himself to build radios and repair anything with electronics in it. He was a proud man but had one weakness; alcohol. He liked it too much and before he was done raising his kids he had fallen into a downward spiral that would cost him his family. Juan's grandmother returned to the island with her kids and decided to go to college and get a degree. Lito was born with a spinal birth defect that prevented him from walking right. It was painful to see him walk but he didn't mind it. He was a vivacious boy. Juan's grandma eventually found a surgeon that corrected his defect and made him walk right. Lito had to be in a back brace for a long time to let the operation heal and he had scars that would last a lifetime. But that did not stop him from growing up into a good looking strong man. His father was too busy drinking and gambling, so Lito had to look for a father figure in his auntie's husband, Edgardo. He taught him work ethics, honesty, and the honor of hard work. Lito turned out to be rebellious, he liked weed, drinking, women, and freedom.

He was a free thinker and a revolutionary of sorts. He had a serious problem with authority and a really short fuse. He started to get into trouble and decided that the best thing for him to do was to join the army. Boy was he mistaken or what? He got in trouble from the word go. The second the sergeant called him a spic he was all over him cursing his mother and everybody in his bloodline for calling Lito a spic. He made it out of basic training on his impressive physical ability alone. The army stationed him in Berlin, of all places. He was doing every drug available on the street every time he went on leave, sometimes waking up in public parks where he had crashed the night before. He was not into hookers, he was very good looking and women fell at his feet wherever he went. The army was a traumatic experience for Lito and it set him on a collision course with all his demons. Lito ended up visiting the stockade frequently and always put up a fight that would leave a couple of mp's bruised up. He would not fight fair either, if there is such a thing. One time he grabbed a beer glass and hit a guy in a club, vertically, not sideways. It fucked him up. Lito surrounded himself with a bunch of Newyorican gangsters that knew martial arts and used them for the sole purpose of beating the crap out of anybody who messed with the crew. His knuckles were blackened from Kung Fu training sessions and bare knuckle street fights. Eventually the army kicked Lito out for insubordination and gave him a dishonorable discharge. When he came out of the army Lito was mentally disturbed, violent, wild. He ended up in every municipal jail in Puerto Rico but managed to get out because a lot of the cops in charge were army veterans themselves or they knew his brother, who was a local drag racing legend. In some occasions they would let him go because his auntie was a prominent politician. Lito developed such a bad reputation that the family would not allow their teenage kids to hang out with him. He was always high and getting into fights. Eventually the police beat Lito up very badly and he ended up getting committed to the hospital and then an asylum for the insane. While being in there he sort of gathered up his thoughts and decided to straighten up his path. He ended up marrying a successful lawyer and moving to the country side where he tended to about 80 acres of mountainous land where he cultivates avocados and plantains. He is the king of the mountain, walking around with his Glock under his shirt and a Heineken in one hand while pulling weeds. He gave Juan a couple of acres to do with them as he pleased. They always talk about how fucked up the world is but end up enjoying how rich and peaceful they have become. Lito is not rich in money, but he does not owe anybody a dime. He's rich in experience and stories to tell his nephew and his grandkids. Juan tells me he's still crazy though, crazy as a fox….

GI JOHNNY

GI Johnny was a daredevil by nature and he somehow ended up in the army. He was always a dangerous guy, not afraid of King Kong if he ever saw him. Ever since high school he would just mind his business and not take shit from anybody. Bullies learned to steer clear of him on account of his cold calculated ruthlessness towards them. In one occasion he pushed a bully down the school stairs after the bully tried to intimidate him. The kid broke his arm and Johnny told him that if he ever tried to fuck with him again he would break his legs and cut his tongue out. The kid never messed with him again. Johnny was a short skinny white kid with no fat on him and nothing but lean muscle. He was built like a pit-bull. He had a 150 IQ and knew how to use it. He liked a challenge and dangerous situations. Everybody in his town knew how crazy he was. One time he climbed a radio tower and zipped down one of the support wires with nothing more than a shirt to protect his hands.

Johnny decided to join the army so he could take advantage of the GI bill to pay for his college. He was first stationed in the US but then was shipped to Germany. While in the US he managed to visit the county jails of 32 different states. Most of the time it was on drunk and disorderly charges or assault on police officers. He always ended up fighting with five or six of them and had all the scars and x-rays to prove it. He loved getting into drinking contests and then getting into fights. Johnny had a fighting spirit like no other, basic training just honed his fighting skills and taught him new ways to hurt people who tried to fuck with him. He had a vicious mouth to go along with his spirit. His mouth always got someone to swing at him, without failing! He was a terror with the ladies too. Wherever he went with his army buddies he ended up taking some married woman to a motel to screw. The locals hated the army boys because they were all in shape, young, and their wives would have flings with them. It was almost comical. When he went to Germany it was just as wild. He loved the brothels and the German open mindedness about sex. He kept doing his stunts until they caught up with him. One night while he was stationed in Germany, he and his buddies decided that they were going to play dare poker in the barracks. Johnny's turn came and he made a bet that he would jump from a training tower forty feet high and take all the cash on the table. The bastard did it and got up and took the money. He bruised his ankles so bad that he stayed in the hospital for a week. They were black and swollen and the pain was unbearable. He was never able to live without pain after that one. Johnny would eat morphine pills, drink alcohol, and do cocaine, like they were going out of style. He cleaned up a little so that he would not get thrown out of the army and eventually made it out with an honorable discharge. He registered at the local university to pursue a career in chemical engineering. He did well but right before graduation he caught a couple of felonies and ruined his career options. Johnny ended up working for a multi-national pharmaceutical before they found out he had a bunch of felonies and fired him. After that he went into crystal meth manufacturing but had to give it up because he became his own best customer. Johnny cleaned up after a couple of suicide by cop attempts failed. He ran into a biker friend who distributed meth for him in the past that had gotten clean. He took Johnny to twelve step programs and Johnny finally decided to give himself a shot and stay clean. About a year after he got clean Johnny got into an auto accident that ruined his lower back and made him go on disability. He could only work part time and sometimes not at all due to the severity of the pain he suffered. While being laid up in bed dealing with one of his pain flare ups, Johnny came up with a chemical formula to turn plastic into petroleum through a complicated process that was sustainable and cheap. It took plastic and submitted it to a heating and evaporative process that yielded petroleum bases along with recycled plastic. The whole process was powered by wind, solar, and methane gas produced by the local dump. It took one gallon of gasoline plus the renewable energy to produce three gallons of fuel. It was revolutionary. The problem was to get the capital needed to develop it in large scale. That's where Juan's rich friends came into play. Juan paid for all the patenting and the lawyers in exchange for a piece of future earnings. The capital funding is still going on and there are talks with big oil companies to buy the patent outright, but Johnny is holding out for a little. He does not want the companies to can his invention so they can keep the world in petroleum slavery. Eventually Johnny will sell it, I think, since he has already released the information about the process's existence to Wiki leaks and the science community. It would be hard to keep it under wraps. Besides, I don't think Johnny wants to be in charge of handling the operational and developmental aspects of the company. He just wants to give his parents a mansion and take good care of them in their last years. And of course he wants to bag as many women as possible before he dies. That I assure you. Johnny is still the ladies man.

JUAN GOES TO ST. MAARTEN

Juan had gone to the Dutch West Indies on a couple of business trips and he liked it. After breaking up with Lucía he decided he needed a change of scenery and pace. St. Maarten was half French and half Dutch and the people were hard working and friendly with an open mind. Prostitution was legal in the Dutch side and that was fine with Juan. He visited the brothels once in a while to get some Colombian girl loving, the best on the planet. These girls were sweet, smart, and eager to please their customers needs. Once in a while he would bring one of them home for the weekend. That's how he met María. They became friends, lovers, almost like two kids with a new toy in a new playground and with no parents to supervise them. They would lay on the beaches of the best resorts of the island and hang out with the superstars. They were like one person, wherever you saw one, you saw the other. Juan and María had something special going. They both wanted María to stop hooking and they got lucky. Juan had met a couple of very rich people while working on their yachts. Juan's mechanical repair abilities had made him a rare commodity on the island. He was the go to guy for trouble shooting mechanical issues, procuring parts, and getting experts to work on the boats. Juan also became the man when it came to getting car parts for people's cars in the island. He had a lot of people in the US who could procure things for him. Eventually Juan and María opened their own yacht and vehicle maintenance company in the island and they lived like kings. They loved going to Divi Little Bay for their lobster bisque and to lay on their chairs and look at the sun dancing on the water. At night they waited for the little sail boat that always anchored about 50 yards from the shore. It was a retired couple from the states who had decided to live in their boat six months out of the year. The other six months they stayed in Saba or the French side, depending on their mood. They had saved enough money to live comfortably and not have to worry about much. The lady, Jenny, was a retired music teacher and Mike was a retired auto mechanic. Juan would work on their boat for free whenever they needed a little repair and María was always hanging out with Jenny, the teacher. Mike and Juan liked to go fishing once in a while, but mostly they liked to sit by Mike's shack by the beach and listen to the Tijuana Brass music and fly with the wind. Juan's stress and anxiety were very low these days, he had arrived at a place in his life where he understood that worrying about money and other stupid stuff did nothing but make him sick. Plus, María was a warrior when it came to taking care of Juan; she pampered him and treated him like a king. One of the owners of the yachts that Juan worked on took a liking to him, María, and their son, so he bought a piece of land and built a house for them to live in. It was on the French side of the island, on a mountain. It was paradise, Juan, María, and their boy. Once every three to six months Brenda would send Daniel (Juan's first son) to spend a week with

Juan in St. Maarten. It was idyllic to see the two little boys playing together. Brenda would come over once a year and stay with Juan and María at their house. She loved it, not a care in the world and the beach, the breeze, the quaint cafes on the French side. Juan ended up building a few huts with all the amenities, so that his friends could come over and stay. It was like their own private little inn. Juan ended up partnering with the rich guy who gave him the land and the house and they bought some more land from a bankrupt resort and built a beautiful resort designed after a Taíno Indian village in his native Island. It became the number one destination for the super rich on the island but Juan always kept a couple of the huts open for his loved ones, Brenda, Lucía, Daniel, his family, and his close friends that were disabled. He still calls me from St. Maarten and asks me to come and stay with him, I go as often as I can. He says one of the huts is mine, along with the land, he even showed me the paperwork. I think I'll retire there.

JUAN GOES TO EUSKADI

Juan had met a bunch of Jai alai players when he was working on cars in Florida. Jai alai was invented by the Basque people, who call the Basque country Euskadi. It is in the north of Spain and south of France. They don't consider themselves Spaniards because they really are not. They are the oldest Europeans and have their own tongue, Euskera, which is a mother tongue, meaning it did not come from any other tongue. Juan's friends took a liking to him for his honesty and willingness to learn their language. Juan also liked their women. His friends, however, warned him about them. Basque women are feisty! But Juan kind of likes that. When Juan finally made a bunch of money he went to visit one of his friends in Euskadi. He had a house by the beach on the Cantabric sea. Juan was immediately enamored with the Basque country, it was heaven; the people, the food, the architecture, the climate, and the women, my God the women! María and Lucía just let Juan play all he wanted, he could not get enough of all these beautiful women, and they could not get enough of him! He decided to buy a little condo by the beach so that he could go and visit once in a while. He loved it so much that when he and María had a daughter they named her Bilbán, in honor of Bilbao. Juan went to see where they manufactured his beloved etorki cheese and also went to see the Jai-Alai games. The Basques invented this game, which was played for royalty and the players all had superstar status. The Basque society was originally matriarchal, but after the Indo-Europeans arrived they forced their patriarchal oppressive ways on the Basque. They heeded their invaders only on the surface, for women are very socially powerful in Euskadi. Juan tells me that his Basque friends all tell him that Christopher Columbus learned of the existence of the new continent from a dying Basque sailor in the Canaries who provided a map. They also told Juan that the Spanish language is nothing but a mixture of Basque and Latin, along with some other dialects. Juan always lights up when he talks about the Basque people, they hold a special place in his heart. They are just like him, strong willed, indestructible, that have been to a thousand wars and will live forever singing the praises of their blood and their mothers...

JUAN LIVES

Juan always tells me that he does not want all the attention his fortune brings him, he just wants to enjoy himself with his family and friends who love him for who he is. He has a soft spot for the disenfranchised, orphans, street people, gypsies, his fellow humans of African descent, and all who make love their priority. He still despises dishonesty but understands that for some people it is impossible to be honest without tearing down the house of cards they built with the blood and sweat of others. He just wished he could lend those people the bravery it takes to tell the truth with peace. He tells me that the system of laws in nations is too dependent on hypocrisy and ignores justice. Juan doesn't understand all the middle eastern based religions and their eternal punishment and violent schemes of fake forgiveness and genocidal classism. Juan refuses to believe that things are just the way they are and that we are all doomed to the status quo. Juan believes in fighting peacefully to the last word, until words are trumped by violence that can only be restrained with targeted and systematic neutralization. He believes in negotiations during or after a fight, and fair ones at that, even for the aggressors. Juan doesn't understand forgiveness without a slap. Juan doesn't understand many things in society, which is why he shuns big cities most of the time. He is tolerant of most modernized humans when they are in play or rest mode but is wary of them when in work mode. Some days he just wants to live by himself on a mountain in the Pyrenees and others he wants to be at a baseball game in Fenway Park. The dichotomy of Juan is never ending. His soul is complex yet simple, profoundly subtle and tender to his loved ones, yet brutally violent against tyrants. The paradox that is Juan and his theories is one that wrenches the stomach with shock and passion, and produces tears of amazement and profound joy. Juan will never waste your time with patronizations for sale, he will slap your face with the truth and let you deal with its consequences. His ferocious journey through his edenic, apocalyptic, phoenixial, and semi-complacent stages reflects the pattern of mankind for millennia. The eternal Apollonian and Dionisic cycles of man in which he must decide where to stand in order to be in peace, all reflect in Juan's life. I thought I was so different than Juan because I didn't experience all his heartbreaks, but I was wrong; Juan lives in me, Juan lives in all of us...

www.ingramcontent.com/pod-product-compliance
Lightning Source LLC
Chambersburg PA
CBHW020245150626
46552CB00020B/387